"I WANT A̶ ... ... ... AS he pulled he̶r̶ ...

"I guess ... ... we've moved beyond the handshake stage," she said, trying to ignore her racing pulse. She was tasting her feminine power, and didn't want to surrender it just yet. She wanted to play a bit, to tease him. "Okay," she said, and bussed him on the cheek.

His eyes lit with warning fire. His gaze brushed her body like a heat wave as he pushed her arms to her sides, leaving her defenseless. "You're asking for it."

Erin's breath caught. "It?" she murmured in an unsteady voice.

He bent closer and tugged her earlobe between his teeth, then released it. "Don't worry. You're gonna get it. And I'll be the one to give it to you. . . ."

# WHAT ARE *LOVESWEPT* ROMANCES?

*They are stories of true romance and touching emotion. We believe those two very important ingredients are constants in our highly sensual and very believable stories in the LOVESWEPT line. Our goal is to give you, the reader, stories of consistently high quality that may sometimes make you laugh, sometimes make you cry, but are always fresh and creative and contain many delightful surprises within their pages.*

*Most romance fans read an enormous number of books. Those they truly love, they keep. Others may be traded with friends and soon forgotten. We hope that each LOVESWEPT romance will be a treasure—a "keeper." We will always try to publish*

*LOVE STORIES YOU'LL NEVER FORGET*
*BY AUTHORS YOU'LL ALWAYS REMEMBER*

The Editors

*Loveswept* ® 648

# DANCE WITH THE DEVIL

## LEANNE BANKS

**BANTAM BOOKS**
*NEW YORK · TORONTO · LONDON · SYDNEY · AUCKLAND*

DANCE WITH THE DEVIL
*A Bantam Book / November 1993*

LOVESWEPT and the wave design are registered
trademarks of Bantam Books, a division of
Bantam Doubleday Dell Publishing Group, Inc.
Registered in U.S. Patent
and Trademark Office and elsewhere.

If you would be interested in receiving protective vinyl covers for your
Loveswept books, please write to this address for information:

Loveswept
Bantam Books
P.O. Box 985
Hicksville, NY 11802

ISBN 0-553-44382-8

Published simultaneously in the United States and Canada

Bantam Books are published by Bantam Books, a division of Bantam Doubleday Dell Publishing Group, Inc. Its trademark, consisting of the words
"Bantam Books" and the portrayal of a rooster, is Registered in U.S. Patent
and Trademark Office and in other countries. Marca Registrada. Bantam
Books, 1540 Broadway, New York, New York 10036.

PRINTED IN THE UNITED STATES OF AMERICA
OPM      0 9 8 7 6 5 4 3 2 1

A special acknowledgment to Susan who said,
"What doesn't kill us makes us stronger."

This is for everyone who couldn't resist the
Pendleton brothers from THE FAIREST OF
THEM ALL. Neither could I!

# ONE

Over the pounding of her heart, Erin Lindsey heard the intruder's footsteps again, but now he was on the front porch. She tightened her grip on the cold shotgun. Her hands were clammy and her knees were trembling. Dear Lord, maybe she had been wrong to move to a horse farm in the middle of Nowhere, Tennessee. What was a woman alone with a six-year-old son doing in this mess?

The door was old, its chain so flimsy that a determined child could probably break it off. She'd arranged for a locksmith to come out to reinforce the door and install new locks. Next week. And she could probably expect the law about the same time. When a crashing noise had awakened her less than half an hour before, she'd immediately called the police, only to learn that the sheriff was on vacation and everyone else was out on a call or needed in town. No help there. She was on her own to take care of herself and her son.

Her skin felt both hot and cold; her breathing was rapid and shallow. Erin was even more frightened than she'd been the last time someone had trespassed on her property. If this was the same person who'd slashed her tires, he was getting bolder. Just moments ago she'd heard the buzz of a motorcycle as it pulled into her driveway. He'd come right up onto her porch now. Heaven only knew what he intended to do. She prayed the shotgun would scare him. It sure scared her.

At the sound of a loud knock she stifled a scream, clutched the gun even more tightly, and backed up against the wall.

"Ms. Lindsey," a gruff male voice called.

Erin didn't say a word; she hardly dared to breathe.

The man knocked again and repeated her name, adding, "I'm one of your neighbors, and—"

"I've got a gun," Erin shouted. She crept to the door, which was flanked by glass panels curtained with lace. She pulled the wispy fabric aside and looked out.

"Ms. Lindsey," the stranger on the porch said, his voice lower, "I live a few miles down the road. The deputy asked me to look in on you."

The October night was Stygian without light from moon or stars, but what Erin could see was not reassuring. The stranger on the porch was huge, a looming dark shadow. A chill ran through her, and she swallowed hard over the knot of fear in her throat. Could this really be a neighbor? She squared her shoulders, reminding herself that it wasn't only her safety she had to think about, but her son's. What would happen to her precious Luke if she made a mistake in trusting this man?

She cleared her throat. "Who exactly sent you over here?"

"Ed Price. Sheriff's out of town, so the office is busy as hell and they don't have a man to spare to send out this way." He paused. "Call Price if it'll make you feel better." His words were clipped and impatient.

"I will." Erin backed all the way to the kitchen. Shaking, she tucked the receiver between ear and shoulder, held the gun in her left hand, and somehow managed to dial the sheriff's office. Within a minute she was assured that her neighbor had been sent. Feeling relieved, she hurried back and opened the door. The man who stepped across her threshold was one of the most intimidating—and blatantly sensual men she'd ever set eyes on.

He wore a black leather jacket that stretched across broad shoulders and jeans that fit his long, muscular legs like a second skin. His features were sharp, and his face wore a grim expression that caused Erin to take a couple of involuntary steps back.

"You okay, Ms. Lindsey?" The man's voice was low and silky, but his eyes looked as cold as chips of ice.

She cleared her throat. "Yes."

Very slowly he eased his palm against the end of the gun she still clutched, and pointed it away from him. "I don't believe we'll be needing this." He pulled the gun from her hands.

Erin instinctively reached for it, then seeing his frown, she folded her arms over her chest. "It's not loaded."

He looked at her as if he thought she had a screw loose. "Then why do you have it?"

She felt defensive. "It looks meaner than I do. Whoever I'm pointing it at doesn't have to know it's empty."

"But if someone comes after you—"

"Mommy! Mommy!" Luke crashed into the back of her legs. "I woke up and couldn't find you."

Erin immediately turned to gather her son into her arms. "It's okay. A neighbor has come by to check on us to make sure we're all right." She squeezed his sturdy, sleep-warm body and mustered a reassuring smile. "And we are. Right?"

Luke peeked over her shoulder, then looked at her with suspicion in his dark eyes. "Why is he holding that gun you told me never, ever, ever to touch? You said I wouldn't be able to sit down for a week if I touched it. Is he gonna get a spanking, Mommy?"

"He's here to help us," Erin explained.

"He looks *mean*," Luke whispered.

Well, she couldn't argue with that. Erin smoothed his cowlick in a gesture of comfort.

The stranger checked the barrel of the gun and propped it against the wall.

"See, Luke, he put the gun down," Erin said. "Let's get you back to bed. You've got to be up early for school."

"When is he leaving?"

"After I go through the barns for your mom." The man didn't smile, but his voice had gentled. "Is there anything you want me to check for you?"

Luke looked thoughtful. "Daisy Mae."

Erin bit her lip to keep from smiling. "Daisy Mae is Luke's chicken."

The man's lips twitched, and for an instant she could almost imagine he was human. "I'll leave a full report with your mom," he said very seriously to Luke.

"Okay, but if you want to look in on Flugie and Chick-chick and—"

"That's enough, Luke. You'll have him stirring up the whole henhouse." Erin glanced at the man. "I'll be right back." She hustled Luke to his bed. It took a few extra kisses and reassuring hugs, but he finally settled down. She grabbed a flashlight from a drawer in the kitchen, locked the front door, and met her neighbor on the porch.

"The horse barn first," he said.

Erin nodded. The night felt like a blanket pulled over her head, with all the darkness and none of the warmth. She concentrated on putting one foot in front of the other, the first fall leaves crunching beneath her steps. "We've got eight brood mares, and all of them are in foal."

"With your acreage you could use two more."

"I know, but you can end up with a real wild card if you use auctions, and I don't know many people around here. So I don't—" Erin stumbled and bumped into him. It was like bumping into a mountain. "Sorry," she mumbled, and walked faster.

That was a mistake. The movement and the darkness disoriented her. She stopped abruptly.

"You coming or not?" he asked, impatience threading his voice again.

She clamped her jaw shut. Lovely man. He had the unique ability to make her feel like used chewing gum left on the pavement. She took a deep breath. "Yes. I just have a little problem with night vision."

She heard him mutter something disparaging. Then he surprised her by putting his hand at the small of her back.

It took her off guard. So far he'd been anything but chivalrous, and she accepted his reluctantly offered assistance. When she became night-blind, her other senses sharpened. *Big hand*, she thought, *to go with the rest of him*. He smelled of leather and faint male muskiness, and his jean-clad thigh was about two inches from hers. She felt a disconcerting ripple of awareness, reminding her she was as much woman as mom and horse-farm owner.

He pressed gently against her back, guiding her forward. A sure touch, she decided, and wondered if he could be gentle with a woman.

"Idiot," she muttered.

"What?"

Her face heated. "Nothing. Here we are." She gave him the keys to unlock the door and stepped away from him.

"How long have you owned Silver Creek?"

"We've been here since August." Erin phrased her answer carefully. She'd learned to be very careful.

"Do you have any extra help, or does your husband—"

"No husband," Erin cut in. Not wanting to explain, she said quickly, "Ed Markham comes every day." Except when he was drunk. Before her neighbor could ask any other questions, she pushed open the door and flicked on a light.

While she headed for the stalls, he walked around the barn, checking it thoroughly until he was satisfied that no one lingered there and nothing had been disturbed. Then he leaned against a beam and watched Erin Lindsey go from stall to stall, murmuring over the horses like a mother to her children.

Nurturing type, he concluded, the kind of woman who would draw men with her delicate femininity. He felt a measure of envy over the layout of her ranch. If he were a nice guy, he'd offer to help. He smiled grimly to himself. Everybody knew he was a moody son of a bitch. The only reason he was here tonight was because he'd had the bad luck of being the one to answer the deputy's phone call when he and his brothers had been watching the ball game. So he was on this mercy mission to Ms. Lindsey, who, in his opinion, had no business operating a horse ranch on her own, especially with only the town drunk as her barn help.

When Erin bent over and her shirt slid up above her hips, he reached another instant conclusion about his neighbor: She had a great rear end.

Natural male instinct had his gaze following the line of her jeans down her long legs, then up again to her thighs. He had a suspicion that Erin Lindsey with the thick, dark eyelashes and big brown eyes had the kind of legs most men would beg to see naked. He shifted. It was a damn shame he'd given up on her type.

She stood, and he noticed the outline of her nipples against the white cotton nightshirt. Her breasts were small, yet very shapely, and the way the tips puckered had his body growing warm.

Shaking his head, he let out a long whoosh of air and forced his attention to her horses. Each of their names was printed below the stalls. "Rapunzel, Snow White, Tinker Bell, Cinderella. You've got some quality hunters, Ms. Lindsey."

Surprised, Erin looked up, searching his face. She'd had a shortage of compliments from men during her life. The dark-haired man was watching her so intently that she looked away. It made her feel strange and self-conscious. "Thank you. I've worked hard."

"But why is this little one named Lily when all the others are named after fairy-tale characters?"

"The others were named by Luke. I named this one because I like lilies. Rapunzel here's got the best bloodlines, though." The mare gave a soft whicker of acknowledgment at the sound of her name. Erin smiled. "She's also the most temperamental."

"Typical of all females," he said dryly.

Erin took exception to that. She wasn't quite sure why, but she suspected he included her in that broad assumption. "If we're going to discuss temperament, then what about studs? They're notorious for being difficult."

A devilish grin lifted the corners of the stranger's mouth. "Why, Ms. Lindsey, everyone knows what drives a stud. As long as he gets it, he's happy."

The sexual tease in his words and tone sent her pulse racing. She had no trouble drawing the correlation between this man and a stud. She took a deep breath and, even though she felt vulnerable, met his gaze steadily. "I know my limitations. There won't be any studs at Silver Creek."

His brows rose, and something flickered in his eyes. Perhaps respect. Perhaps not, she thought more realistically. She prided herself on being realistic, if little else.

He shifted, then deliberately looked around the barn. It was a fragile moment; he'd seen that look of sexy confusion flash over her face. Intentional or not, she was seductive. His body tightened in a subtle, but unmistakable way, and he suddenly had the alien impulse to befriend this woman.

"I can introduce you to a reliable guy who might have a mare or two he'd like to sell."

Erin studied him. He was big and all his edges were rough. His hair was black and cut in a don't-give-a-damn style. The ends would have fallen over his collar if he'd been wearing a shirt with one instead of a black T-shirt under his leather jacket. His eyes were a strange blue, almost violet, his mouth firm and unsmiling. Sexy and stand-offish at the same time, he reminded her of an arrogant tomcat—or that moody stud that had been the subject moments ago. Other women would be tempted to try to soften that brooding aura and domesticate him—*other women*, being the operative words.

He put her warning signals on full alert. She'd be a fool to trust him. "Why would you be willing to help?" she finally asked.

He shrugged. "You're new here. We're neighbors. I'll be starting my own operation within a year or so."

Despite her doubts and reservations about him,

she was curious and a little fascinated, so she dared to ask, "Why are you waiting?"

His jaw tightened. "My oldest brother's in charge of the farm. He wants to wait a little longer before we get into the horse business."

"You don't sound happy about it," she ventured.

"I'm not," he said shortly. His relationships with members of his family except his sister were touchy. Prodding these sore points made him restless—and in the past restlessness had driven him to do things best left undone. Abruptly he moved away from the wall. "So how about it? You want to meet this guy or not?"

Erin paused, still hesitant. But she nodded. "Okay."

They locked up and checked the hay barn. Then he managed to look in on the chickens without causing a single cluck. His movements were quiet and coordinated.

"They were all sleeping," he said when he shut the pen. "Which one was Daisy Mae?"

"The fattest one."

He nodded in understanding and again put his hand at the back of her waist, guiding her toward the house. "You'd better check your fences tomorrow. And your feed."

"I will," Erin said, adding it to her list of three hundred other things to do. "I wonder what exactly woke me."

"Did you hear any voices?"

"No. Just a crashing sound, then nothing." She turned to him. "Sorry to get you—" She tripped again.

"Hold it." He caught her easily, his hand clasping her rib cage while he pulled her against him, his thigh wedged between her legs.

Her heart slammed in her chest and she fought to catch her breath. "I should come with a warning label: 'Beware, clumsy.'" She stepped back, and stumbled again, stomping on what felt like the toe of his boot. "I'm sorry."

He swore under his breath, then in one smooth motion he lifted her off the ground. Erin gasped. The flashlight in her hand waved wildly, its beam arcing first to the sky, then to the ground. She was too aware of the strength of this man's arms, the power of his chest beneath her hands, and the warmth of his breath on her cheek. A dizzy, desperate feeling hummed in her blood. She strained against it. "This really"—she took a breath—"really isn't necessary."

"Maybe," he admitted. "But it's a hell of a lot easier than picking you up off the ground every other step."

Embarrassed, she bit her lip. "I said I was sorry."

He reached the porch and looked down at her. She felt the searing intensity of his violet gaze all the way to her heart and hoped he wasn't nearly as perceptive as he appeared to be.

Her body stiffened in his arms, and he saw the self-conscious flush color her cheeks. He eased her to her feet, but when she would have turned away, he caught her chin. "No problem. You're no hardship to hold, Erin."

She stared at him, feeling her nerve endings jump. She didn't need this. She absolutely did not need this. Resolutely lifting her chin, Erin stepped away from him. "Well, thank you for coming." She backed up another step so that she wouldn't feel his body heat. "I'm sorry the deputy got you out here for nothing."

He shrugged off her apology. "You'll give my report to your son."

Erin smiled. "Of course."

"So he'll know that *mean* man kept his word," he said pointedly.

Erin winced. "Children can be very..." She searched for the right word.

"Honest."

"Yes. Luke doesn't hold back." She chuckled, remembering a recent war they'd had over dinner. "I fixed a casserole the other night and he let me know exactly what he thought of it."

"Uh-huh. Bet it was tuna."

"How did you know?"

"Masculine intuition." His tone was serious. His expression was not.

"Thought there was only feminine intuition," she countered.

"But I'm not feminine." His voice was silky soft.

Erin swallowed, reminding herself she was chatting with the human equivalent of the big bad wolf. "I, uh, already guessed that."

He took a step closer and watched her take a step back. If he were a gentleman, he'd give her some space and say good night. But he was no gentleman. Besides, stirring up Erin Lindsey was fun. "So when are you gonna spank me?"

Erin just gaped at him. The man was outrageous. And he made her nervous as hell. "The rules are a little different for big boys," she managed. "Besides you don't strike me as the type to let *anyone* get the best of you."

There was that sexy grin of his again. "Ms. Lindsey, I always give my best."

She'd just bet he "gave his best"—to any and every willing woman in the county. Erin shook her head and let out a shaky sigh. "I'm sure you do. Thank you again for coming by," she said politely, but clearly dismissing him.

He nodded, a knowing glint in his eyes. "Welcome to Beulah County, Ms. Erin Lindsey. I'll stop by tomorrow and we can set up a time to visit that horse owner I was telling you about."

"Good." She watched him saunter down the steps to his big black bike. He picked up the helmet, placed it on his head, and mounted the bike.

"I never caught your name," she called.

"Pendleton. Garth Pendleton." He started the

engine and gave her a quick nod, then started down the driveway.

For a full minute Erin stared after him. *Garth Pendleton. Garth Pendleton. Garth Pendleton.* It couldn't be!

She shook her head. Of all the sick coincidences in the world. Could it *really* be a coincidence? The most terrifying and devastating moments of her life flashed before her with sharp, painful clarity. She felt the fear, grief, and guilt as if it had just happened. She closed her eyes against the truth.

God help her. Garth Pendleton was the man who'd killed her father.

# TWO

By three o'clock the following afternoon, Erin had
received more visitors and calls in one day than she'd
received the entire time she'd been in Beulah County.
The first to stop by was a tall, peppy, dark-haired
woman who introduced herself as Carly Bradford.
Carly had come with a plate of chocolate chip cookies
and complimentary tickets for a kiddie cruise on her
riverboat in hand.

During their brief conversation Erin learned Carly
was the youngest sister to seven brothers, one of whom
was Garth. But that wasn't really a surprise to Erin,
because she'd been fascinated by how similar Carly's
blue-violet eyes were to Garth's.

Erin wondered if Carly knew her brother had killed
a man.

*In self-defense*, her conscience reminded her.

No sooner had Carly gone than another car pulled

into the driveway. Mrs. Whitman brought an apple pie and apologized profusely for not visiting earlier. She told Erin about the children's Sunday school classes at the local church and invited her to attend. She thanked the older woman, but she didn't make any promises.

Erin was feeling very nervous by the time a lady who identified herself as Augusta Winfree telephoned. Augusta's warmth quickly put Erin at ease, and she was intrigued—but apprehensive—about the invitation extended to bring Luke to the October carnival with a special group of children—children who had lost a parent.

Erin was sweeping the barn, trying to decide how to deal with the visitors and callers and their well-intended invitations, when Luke burst into the barn.

"Hey, Mom! That man who helped us last night, the one I thought was mean, well, he's here. And he's got a motorcycle!" His face flushed with excitement, he bounced up and down. "I asked him if I could ride it and he said I had to get per- per-"

"Permission."

"Yeah. Can I go now?"

Erin shook her head, feeling her stomach churn at the prospect of seeing Garth Pendleton again. "I don't think that's a good idea, Luke. Motorcycles can be very dangerous." *To say nothing of the man driving it.*

"But, Mom," Luke protested.

Erin yanked off her gloves, but deliberately softened her voice. She didn't want to take her nerves out on Luke. "We'll discuss it later, honey."

"Aw, mom—"

A shaft of sunlight spilled through the barn as the door was pushed farther open. No jacket today, Erin observed, taking in the impressive sight of Garth Pendleton. Just a navy T-shirt, clean denims, and boots. He carried a magazine. She should say something, she thought, but words fled her mind. She could only stare at his eyes, his incredible eyes—definitely not the eyes of a killer. The eyes of a lover? The thought put her emotions in an uproar.

"Busy day," Garth said, looking at the broom and her discarded gloves. "Where's Ed?"

"He took off some extra time after lunch. He'll be back tomorrow."

"Ed's been known to tilt the bottle too much at times."

"I'm sure we'll be fine."

Garth narrowed his eyes at her tone. She'd been scared last night, understandably scared, but he knew he'd felt a kick of mutual awareness. Today she seemed tense and distant.

"She won't let me ride the motorcycle," Luke announced despondently.

Garth shrugged and moved closer to Luke. "She's the boss. Maybe she'll let you go to the carnival instead. Did Augusta call?"

Erin nodded. "Yes, but I really hadn't—"

"A carnival," Luke interrupted, his face brightening. "When will it be? Can we go?"

Feeling a double jab of guilt and frustration, Erin knelt down to her towheaded son who'd missed too much in his young life and put her hands on his shoulders. "I just found out about the carnival today, honey. It's in two weeks, but it's at night."

Luke's face fell. "We can't go."

His disappointment pulled at her, and she shook her head. "I didn't say that."

"Yeah, but we never go anywhere at night." Luke kicked at the ground. "And we don't know anybody who could take us."

Garth supposed it wouldn't kill him to take them. He could borrow Daniel's car. "I could take you."

Erin shook her head. "That's not necessary," she said quickly and stood. Lord, this was getting complicated. How could she manage to keep Luke happy *and* keep a low profile for a little longer? And how could she avoid Garth Pendleton, a man who could ruin their chances for a fresh start?

Erin sighed, ruffling Luke's hair between her fingers. "I guess if I called Augusta, she'd be able to suggest something."

"So, we're gonna go! Yahoo!" Luke screamed.

"I think we can manage. Now, go back to the house and finish the milk and cookies I set out for you."

After Luke ran out of the barn, sudden quiet settled heavily. Garth was studying her . . . and making her too aware of him. Uneasiness spurred her into action, and she picked up the broom.

"Taking you and Luke to the carnival isn't a problem," he said.

He was being kind, and she didn't want his kindness. She didn't want to believe that he could be kind. She just wanted him to leave her alone. "It was nice of you to offer." She shut a stall door. "But I'm sure you've got better ways to spend your Saturday nights."

She took a deep breath and unnecessarily hit the stall door again, then walked toward the barn door. "I thought about what you said—adding a couple more mares. I've decided I'd rather wait on that. Thanks anyway, though."

Garth didn't say anything. As the silence lengthened, Erin grew so curious about his reaction that she couldn't resist looking over her shoulder at him. He was two steps behind her, and she wasn't fooling him one bit, she realized. He knew she was acting strangely. She could tell by the skeptical look on his face.

"Okay," he said, wondering why Erin seemed so upset. Had one of Beulah County's fine citizens educated her about the Pendleton Devil? Maybe someone had told her he was a ladies' man, or that he occasionally drank too much, or that he had the ability to break a man's neck in five seconds flat—no, not that last one. There were plenty of rumors, but no one in town *knew* about that last one.

He took a deep breath. "It looked like somebody ran into your mailbox, so I fixed it this morning."

"My mailbox? I didn't notice it."

Crossing his arms over his chest, he leaned against the wall and looked down at her. "That must have been what you heard last night, somebody plowing into it."

Erin was too distracted to think about the mailbox, or last night, or much of anything else at the moment except Garth. She was absorbed by his sleek looks, his sexy strut, and those violet eyes that didn't miss a thing. More disconcerting was the way her blood seemed to pop and sizzle when he stood close to her. Why now? And for Pete's sake, *why him*?

Erin gave herself a hard mental shake and tried for a polite smile. "It seems I owe you another thank-you."

For an instant his eyes went colder than a morgue. Her heart jumped into her throat, and she took a step back.

"I don't collect debts," he said, his voice rough and soft as a kitten's tongue. "I'm a simple man. Thank-you and a handshake will do."

She felt a shot of apprehension, yet at the same time she didn't want to be rude. "Thank you," she whispered.

Garth nodded, extending his hand and watching her carefully.

Erin stared at it, hesitating. His palm was calloused, the fingers long and supple. He leaned closer, and she was mesmerized. She lifted her hand and slid it into his. His palm swallowed hers in a firm embrace. She sucked in a deep breath and looked up, compelled to meet his gaze. She felt the rasp of his callouses, the contained strength of his grip. His thumb rubbed the inside of her wrist, sending her pulse skittering.

It was odd, Garth thought, the way touching her hand made him wonder what the rest of her felt like. Her hands were small, soft, and fair with a few callouses. Tender, but firm like her nature, he guessed.

He saw the woman's need flash through her brown eyes, the fight to tamp it down, and felt a corresponding tightening inside him. If he were a less selfish man, he'd step away and free her from the spell being woven between them, but he felt too greedy—greedy in a way he couldn't remember being before. Greedy for someone soft and real. So he pushed his luck and cocked his head to one side, watching her while he turned their hands and laced his fingers through hers.

Erin sensed the edge of recklessness in him. The brush of his rough hands against the soft, vulnerable inner part of her fingers felt oddly intimate and exciting. It made her think of other places where he was rough and she was soft.

Then he lifted their hands to his lips and pressed an open-mouth kiss to the inside of her wrist.

Erin gasped and jerked back. She had the oddest thought—that she'd just shaken hands with the devil and gotten burned.


He'd be damned if he set foot on Erin Lindsey's ranch again. Swearing a blue streak, Garth came to a squealing halt at the stop sign. After looking both ways, he gunned the Harley's engine and roared onto the main road.

His heavy-handed move on Erin had scared her spitless, and he had no idea why he'd done it except to see if the warm woman he'd met last night existed somewhere inside the cool one he'd confronted today. He scowled, wondering why he gave a damn. Taking that equestrian journal to her had been as stupid as bringing flowers would have been. After she'd jerked her hand away as if he were going to attack her, he'd thrust the magazine at her and hauled butt out of her barn.

He opened the throttle and nudged the speed up to eighty. He wasn't sure why he'd felt an immediate and compelling interest in the woman anyway. The combination of fear and determination in her? The way she'd comforted her son?

Could be he liked the way her slight body had felt in his arms . . . her feminine scent. Could be he was thinking below his waist instead of with his brain.

He cursed again, dismissing the physical attraction. Erin was straight and slim, when he'd always dated curvy women with hearts made of stainless steel. The one woman he'd thought he loved had completely fooled him. When she'd gotten pregnant with his baby, she'd gotten rid of it instead of marrying him. Garth remembered her words: "It's been fun, Garth, but a baby would mess up my plans." She'd taught him a lesson he would never forget.

Bitter and restless, he'd left college and taken off for Denver. *Denver*. The mere thought of the city made his stomach turn. And it had all started because of a woman.

His sister, Carly, would say he'd always gotten involved with the *wrong* kind of woman. She said he needed someone with "real heart." Every once in a while he wondered about that theory, then he recalled that women with "real heart" all but hid behind their mothers' skirts when he came around. They probably sensed his black soul, he decided grimly and downshifted as he rounded a turn.

Pulling into the lane leading to his brother Daniel's house, Garth felt a sense of familiarity, but no sense of belonging. The large white farmhouse, bordered by three tall oaks on one side and a lush weeping willow on the other, had housed four generations of

Pendletons. He'd grown up in this house with his sister and six brothers, but somehow, it didn't seem to be his. Nothing seemed to be his.

Garth stopped the Harley and pulled off his helmet, relishing the warmth of the sun on his head. Erin had a great piece of land, good solid stock, and too much to handle. She was going to ruin it if she didn't get better help. He tried to persuade himself that her horse farm was the basis of his interest in her; it was just a reminder of what he didn't have. And how damned tired he was of waiting for Daniel to give the go-ahead on the horse business.

He mentally wiped his hands of Erin and her problems. He had enough problems of his own.

Taking a break from cleaning stalls, Erin leaned against the shovel and hummed along with the love song playing on the radio.

"One-two-three. One-two-three," she counted, and tried to move her feet in rhythm.

Every couple of months in the privacy of her home, Erin attempted to dance. A fruitless endeavor, but she kept hoping something would change, that her feet would catch the rhythm that played in her mind, that her hips would move gracefully. She wanted to be able, metaphorically, to stick out her tongue at that old witch who'd taught dance lessons at the girls' school she'd attended. "Hopeless," Miss Snyder had said. "You're completely hopeless." Unfortunately she'd been humiliatingly correct so far.

Dancing was her secret escape hatch when it seemed like the world was racking up points against her. She remembered being seventeen, alone, and six months pregnant, trying to dance in her room in that unwed-mothers' home. And during labor, whenever the nurse left her alone in the room, Erin had fought the fear by trying to do a slow foxtrot. Then there were the sleepless nights when she'd held Luke and tried to dance away his colic.

Frowning in concentration, Erin moved awkwardly, leaned too far to the right, and stepped on her own toes, and the frustration of the last week hit her hard.

"Darn it!" she yelled, throwing the shovel to the ground. The disheartening conversations played through her mind.

*"Miz Lindsey, I broke my leg and won't be able to work for a while,"* Ed Markham had said four days ago.

*"No, Mommy. Nothing's wrong,"* Luke said every afternoon at the bus stop. But his voice was unsteady, and he avoided meeting her gaze. Something was wrong. He'd been quiet the last few days, and Erin was so tired every evening that she felt guilty he was being deprived of something he needed—such as a Daddy, or her undivided attention, or something else she couldn't name.

And Garth Pendleton had preyed on her mind.

She knew the whole story about her father's death; he'd gone nuts and shot a man, then turned his gun on Garth. Garth had killed him in self-defense.

She'd been able to place part of the blame on Garth—until meeting him. He was real and human and that wasn't easy to deal with.

Erin would love to blame Garth or someone else, but she absolutely couldn't. The reason her father had gone around the bend was something she would carry until the day she died. *She* had caused his death. Her chest ached when she thought of it, and lately she'd thought of it too often—along with the futile wish that she could have done something to prevent it.

The distant sound of an engine interrupted her thoughts, and she checked her watch. Time to pick up Luke at the bus stop. Erin pushed her brooding thoughts to the back of her mind, propped the shovel against the wall, and hurried out of the barn.

She came to a dead halt. Garth Pendleton roared in on his bike with *her son* behind him. Her heart seemed to skip a beat.

Garth stopped the bike, lifted Luke to the ground, and saw Erin. She appeared to be frozen in place. He pulled the too-big helmet off of Luke's head, and the boy ran to his mother.

"Mom! Garth's motorcycle is so cool!"

Garth watched Erin catch Luke in her arms. Her

gaze spit nails at him over the boy's shoulder. The corners of his mouth lifted ironically. He wasn't any happier about his presence here than she was.

*Mama Bear and her cub*, he thought, idly wondering what it would take to get Mama Bear to share some of her honey with him. She'd probably scratch out his eyes first. It didn't take a genius to see that the two of them were close, and the sight of those two blond heads together made him feel a ridiculous twinge of envy.

Erin deliberately ignored the grin Garth tossed her. She hugged Luke, then pulled back to look at her little boy. "I told you I didn't want—" She stopped, and the lecturing note vanished from her voice as she noticed his torn shirt and swollen eye. "What on earth has happened to you?"

Not meeting her gaze, Luke began to dance beneath her hands. "Well, Bobby Davidson sorta hit me."

"Hit you?"

Luke ducked his head. "Yeah. He's been making fun of me all week."

"But why did he hit you?" *Making fun*. It tore at her heart. Children could be so ruthless. Erin looked from Luke to Garth.

Garth shrugged off the demand for explanation in her gaze. He didn't want to interfere. He just wanted to leave. He'd sworn not to set foot on Erin Lindsey's land again, yet here he was.

Luke lowered his voice. "I told him he was a pumpkin puke sucker."

Garth bit his lip at the colorful expression.

Erin was aghast. "Luke, you know better than to call people names. Why in the world did you do that?"

"He called me a little sissy klutz," he mumbled.

Erin winced. She wished she could have taken the insults and punches for Luke. "Oh, no," she whispered, and hugged him close. She nodded in understanding and sighed. "You're no sissy, but you got my genes when it comes to grace, honey. Let's get some ice on that eye. You'll probably have a shiner, and we'll talk about name-calling later." She threw a worried glance at Garth. "Please wait just a minute. I'll be right back."

Garth watched them go and shoved his hands into his pockets. Hell, he ought to get on his bike and leave. He'd done his good deed for the day by scaring the pumpkin puke out of Bobby Davidson and safely delivering Luke to his mom. If he kept up this good-deed stuff, someone might get wind of it and actually expect him to keep it up. Imagine that. What would the fine citizens of Beulah County do if they heard *good* rumors about the Pendleton Devil?

He'd about convinced himself to leave when Erin walked back, rubbing her forehead. Garth thought she looked exhausted.

"I don't know what to say except thank you." She

lifted her hands in distress. "I was leaving to pick him up when you drove into the yard. The bus must have come a little early, or my watch must be a little slow."

Garth saw that Erin tended to talk a mile a minute when she was upset. He opened his mouth to respond, but she kept on.

Erin shook her head, pacing back and forth. "I knew something was wrong. I should have done something. I should have—"

"You want me to get the shovel for you?" he cut in. Garth had made enough mistakes in his life to be well acquainted with the useless exercise of guilt. Yes, even a devil could feel guilt. He'd spent countless hours second-guessing the most difficult, instinctive choice of his life, the choice to end another man's life. He couldn't explain why, but he didn't like seeing Erin carry such a burden.

She blinked. "Shovel?"

"So you can dig a hole for you and your guilt to crawl into?"

Erin took a deep breath and a half moment's pause. But then the mothering part of her mind searched out ways she could have prevented the incident. "But maybe I could have—"

"You couldn't have done a damn thing. The bus was early. Boys get into fights." He gave a dry laugh. "Considering Luke is only in first grade, I'm impressed with his creativity."

Erin was silent for a long moment, then her lips twitched in secret amusement. "Pumpkin puke sucker?"

Oddly pleased that he'd teased out that smile, Garth said, "Hey, it was more original than what Bobby said."

Her smile fell. "Yeah, but Bobby was right about Luke's coordination. Since he started walking, he's worn bruises every day of his life. He's a fairly good rider, but as soon as those feet hit the ground . . ." She shrugged.

Garth leaned against the big oak and considered her problem. She wore her hair loose today. The wind was playing with it, brushing it against her chin. Her straight blond hair looked soft, her skin did too. And her lips reminded him of a ripe plum, lush and tender.

For a moment he wished Erin Lindsey was one of those women with stainless-steel hearts. He wished she was a bad girl. Then he'd have no compunction about finding out if her mouth tasted as good as it looked or how she liked a man to touch her. He exhaled in frustration and shook his head. He was crazy.

"Have you tried organized sports?"

She swept her hair behind her ear. "When we were in—" Realizing what she was about to reveal, she caught herself. "Before we came here, Luke was too young. I heard about soccer too late. It had already started."

Noting the pause, Garth narrowed his eyes. He'd figure it out later. "Softball?" he asked.

Erin grimaced. "I've tried to help him, but it's like the blind leading the blind. It's a wonder we don't hurt each other." A horrible thought struck her. "Lord, I hope he doesn't have the same problem with dancing that I do." She looked up at Garth and, seeing his confused expression, she felt a rush of self-consciousness. "Just forget I said that."

"Dancing?"

Erin shook her head. "Long story," she said, wishing she'd kept her mouth shut. "Old story." She caught the light of amusement in his eyes and muttered, "Stupid story."

"I'd love to hear it." His voice was deep, sexy, seductive—and entertained.

Erin rolled her eyes. She should have known he wouldn't do the polite thing and drop the uncomfortable subject. She pressed her lips together and crossed her arms for lack of anything else to do.

"I have a hunch that I won't get it out of you today." His gaze flicked over her. "I can tell that with you torture and seduction won't work."

"You mean they're not the same?" It was out before she realized it. She saw his eyes darken and felt a corresponding ripple run through her nether regions.

"All depends on your definition of torture. Different strokes"—he paused meaningfully and gave her a lazy grin—"for different folks." Then he shrugged as if he were no threat. "I'm flexible."

Erin tore her gaze from his. Garth Pendleton was a menace. He made her blush. He made her say things she shouldn't. He made her feel things she had no business feeling. When she was around him, she didn't know whether she was coming or going. Going sounded good right now. "I think—"

Garth saw the dismissal coming and cut it off. "Back to Luke's problem. Have you thought about martial arts?"

Erin blinked, then shook her head. "No." Switching gears again, she instinctively rejected the idea of martial arts. "I don't want Luke thinking that the best way to settle an argument is with a karate kick."

"Martial arts isn't supposed to teach that. A student learns self-discipline, appreciation for his environment, and self-confidence." He took in her skeptical expression. "It's also great for coordination."

"I don't know." Still reluctant, Erin thought of the possibility that she'd have to drive at night, which was hard for her because of her problem with night vision. "Where's the karate club?"

"The nearest club is thirty miles away, but the guy's a great teacher."

"Do you have any idea when the classes are held?"

"Probably afternoon and evening," he replied, wondering what was bothering her.

Erin shook her head in disappointment. "Afternoons might work, but I can't do the night driving. And there's no one to car-pool with." She tried for a smile. "Thanks for the suggestion, though."

"Maybe—" he said, then immediately nixed the idea that nudged at him.

Erin looked up expectantly, her warm brown eyes focused completely on him. "Maybe what?"

Garth felt a sinking sensation. She might be slim as a reed and a mom to the core, certainly no vamp, but when Erin Lindsey gazed at him as she did now, he felt like tearing off his shirt and beating his chest. She looked like someone who'd lost one too many of her dreams, and he found himself wanting to give them back. He shouldn't do it. He shouldn't. He should let Erin take care of her own problems.

"I could teach him."

The blood drained from her face, and Erin took a step back. She felt as if the bottom had fallen out of her stomach. For a moment her underlying uneasiness had hovered like a vague cloud, but with Garth's offer to teach Luke karate, painful reality sliced through her. She knew Garth had killed her father with a martial-arts move that had worked with deadly precision. His expertise repelled her. At the same time, she realized, he would have been killed if he hadn't used that expertise.

Garth eyed her strangely, then gave a careless shrug. "Hey, listen, it was only an idea. If it bothers you that much—"

"No." Erin held up a hand. "It's just . . ." Of course it bothered her! But how could she could explain her reaction without revealing who she was and who her father was. She'd vowed to leave all that behind in Denver. If she and Luke were going to get the fresh start they needed, then she had to keep her mouth shut. She closed her eyes for a moment. "It's been a rough week," she said lamely, explaining nothing.

"I heard about Ed Markham." It wasn't "I told you so," but it was close.

Erin opened her eyes, frustrated and confused. Confusion seemed to be a permanent state around Garth Pendleton. "Why?" she asked bluntly. "Why are you offering to help with Luke?"

Garth frowned, shifting his stance. He was uncomfortable justifying his actions. "I'll be starting my own operation soon. Until then I've got some time on my hands, and Luke seems like a good kid." Then he felt like he was selling Erin on the idea and he got irritated. "If you've got to grill me about it, forget it." He started to leave.

"Would you wait a minute?" She matched him glare for glare. "You have to admit it's not a fair trade. You're not getting anything out of this."

"I've covered this ground with you before."

Erin remembered—*a simple thank-you and a handshake*. For many reasons, though, a thank-you and a handshake weren't so simple with Garth.

"It's still not equitable."

Garth moved closer until he was a half step away from her. Erin's pulse tripped over itself. "Do you argue with everyone, or am I special? If you're so worried about me getting something out of this arrangement, give me some time." His hot, quick, potent gaze swept over her. "I'll think of something."

# THREE

She was surrounded, Garth observed, looking at the cluster of men buzzing around Erin as if she were a flower ripe for pollination.

A surge of jealousy came out of nowhere and hit him broadside. He muttered a curse under his breath, then remembered he was in church for the first time in six years. Of course he could be struck by lightning for his transgressions. No lightning this time, he thought grimly, watching Erin smile at Ben Centrell. Just lust.

Garth ignored the whispers and stares, although he could imagine they were saying plenty about the Pendleton Devil. They probably wondered where his pitchfork was, he thought, feeling a kick of dark amusement. He made his way to the front of the church where Erin was getting ready to take a seat.

"How long have you been in Beulah County, Erin?" Garth heard Ben ask.

"Since August. And you?"

"Oh, I'm a hometown boy." Ben gave her a big smile. "I know this county like I know the back of my hand. If you need anything, anything at all, you just give me a holler."

Garth scowled. He'd bet Ben would be willing to take care of "anything at all" when it came to Erin's needs. Years ago, when he was fifteen, Garth had accepted a stupid dare to take Ben's daddy's car for a joyride. Right now he was wishing he'd wrecked it.

"So, where are you from?" Ben asked Erin. "Do you have any family in Tennessee? Is that why you came here?"

Garth was interested in the answers too. In the past two weeks he'd noticed Erin wasn't exactly forthcoming about her past. He'd found himself burning with curiosity.

"We lived out west," she answered stiffly. "No family. Just Luke and me, and the horses and the chickens."

"Out west" could mean she'd lived almost anywhere. His instincts told him she was trying to hide something. When Ben looked ready to grill her some more, Garth toyed with the idea of allowing it, but an odd protective feeling nagged at him, and he decided to get his own answers later . . . in private.

"How's your father doing?" Garth asked Ben, then murmured an "excuse me," and moved to Erin's side.

Ben's eyes widened. "Well, if it isn't the black sheep of the Pendletons. I figured the only way I'd see you in church again would be for your funeral."

"Yeah, well, I decided to show up early," Garth muttered. He turned his attention to Erin. "Where's Luke?"

"Children's church." She felt the tug and pull of relief and excitement at Garth's presence.

Ben leaned forward. "Has anyone warned you about this guy?" he asked Erin in a semijoking tone.

Garth would have loved to stuff a hymnal down Ben's throat. He stiffened, waiting for Erin's response.

She frowned. No one *had* to warn her. "Garth has helped me with the horses since my barn help broke his leg." She thought about the time Garth had spent with Luke. "He's been very generous."

Ben blinked, then cleared his throat. "Hey, if you needed help, you should have called—" The organ began playing.

"Oh, there's the music," Erin murmured, looking from Ben to Garth, unable to decide what to do with them. They were both disturbing. Ben asked questions she didn't want to answer, and Garth made her feel things she didn't want to feel. *Talk about being caught between the devil and the deep blue sea.* "I guess it's time to sit down." When nobody moved, she lifted her shoulders uncertainly. "It's nice meeting you, Ben."

Ben paused, shot Garth a disgruntled look, and favored Erin with another grin. Then he sauntered to the back of the church.

"Sonova—"

Erin's wide-eyed glance cut him off.

"Sorry. Like Ben said, I haven't been to church in a long time."

She sat down and crossed her legs. "That makes two of us," she murmured under her breath.

Pocketing that fact in the back of his mind, Garth took a long slow look at Erin. Her dress had little blue flowers on it with lace at the top and bottom. The last cloth-covered button left a gap of several inches before the bottom of the dress, and his gaze caught on the span of silk-covered flesh just above her knees.

Her legs were lithe and feminine, yet Garth knew they were strong. He'd watched her ride the horses. He looked at the shapely calves and wanted to skim his hands over them, then nudge the blue pumps off her feet.

He wondered if she wore stockings or pantyhose. Erin was such a dichotomy. She worked hard all day, but somehow managed to look feminine at the same time. It was the little things, he decided. Like the fact that she always wore lipstick and a soft, floral perfume with just a hint of spice. When she pulled her hair into a ponytail, she tied it with a ribbon. He glanced at her thigh and thought he saw a small bump raising the material. A garter. He felt a slow swell of heat.

She grazed his arm with her hand, and his head whipped up.

Erin smiled. "You still haven't answered my question."

*Because I've been too busy planning how to get you out of those stockings so that I can get between your thighs.* Garth shook his head. If he wasn't headed for hell because of his past, then he was for what he was thinking about Erin. "What did you ask?"

"Why haven't you been to church in a long time?"

Uncomfortable, he shrugged. "Guess I had to make peace with myself."

Erin tensed, a flurry of emotion reminding her of her own lack of peace. Underneath that shrug, past his bitter, moody exterior, how had he handled killing her father? Did he ever feel guilty? "And have you made peace with yourself?"

He narrowed his eyes. "I'm working on it. How about you?"

She glanced away, feeling a hollow ache and wishing for something she couldn't have, particularly from him: compassion, understanding. She pressed her lips together and, sensing the intensity of his gaze, she looked back at him. "I guess I'm working on it too," she whispered, then turned her attention to the service.

Garth watched her, not knowing what had saddened her. He saw her short nails biting into her small clenched hands and felt an urge to put his hand over hers, but restrained himself. Somehow he could taste the sense of regret she was experiencing.

A connection was made. It took him off guard

because he'd never felt it before. Something right when it had always been something wrong. He felt the click inside him so strongly, he wondered if she heard it too.

They looked like candidates for a Laurel and Hardy movie, Garth decided as he watched Erin throw a softball to Luke. The pitch was wide, but Luke was game. Erin's great tush was poked out in an attention-getting position. Luke leaned a little too far to the left and ended up eating fallen leaves. Erin ran to pick him up.

Garth almost laughed. He'd promised Luke another karate lesson, but as Erin had said, Luke could use some help with baseball too. "Can you use another player?" he called, walking toward them.

Erin spun around and smiled. "I don't know. This is amateur hour."

He noticed her ambivalence toward him. That ambivalence was always there and it irritated the hell out of him. "I'm no pro," Garth said, pushing her to invite him to stay.

"Yeah, but I bet you're a lot better than we are," Luke said.

"Exactly." Erin flicked a leaf off Luke's head. Just by sitting beside her in church today, Garth had played havoc with her emotions; she wished he were a hundred miles away, but she knew Luke was thrilled to see him. She sighed. "What do you say? You think we should let him play?"

"Sure!" Luke scratched his ear. "He can show me how to swing, since you don't know how."

Erin raised her hands in surrender. "Okay. I know when I'm beat. I'll pitch and you two bat."

Garth wished the mother would exhibit half the enthusiasm for his presence the son did. He had the urge to toss Erin Lindsey over his shoulder, head for the nearest cave, and give her his undivided attention.

Instead he strolled over to home plate and positioned himself behind Luke. "You ready to hit a home run? Choke up on the bat, slugger." He crouched over, placing his hands on either side of Luke's on the wooden bat. "That's right. You want me to do it with you this first time?"

Luke nodded. "Yeah, but then I want to do it by myself."

Garth looked at Erin. "He's definitely your son."

Erin glanced at him curiously. "Why do you say that?"

"He's got the same blond hair, same big brown eyes, same deadly charm." Garth ruffled Luke's hair, then lifted a dark eyebrow. "And he's independent as—" He caught himself just in time. Damn. He wasn't used to watching his language.

"As all get out," Erin generously said with a sassy wink.

"Yeah," he responded suggestively, and watched her gaze skitter away from his.

Luke shifted impatiently. "Talk, talk, talk. When are we gonna play?"

"Now. Put it right over the plate, Erin, and not too high."

"Right, Mom," Luke echoed. "Right over the plate."

Seeing them gaze at her expectantly did something to Erin's heart. It reminded her of all Luke had missed by not having a father around. It made her think of how much he admired Garth, and the danger in getting attached to him.

And it brought to mind how, after church, when she'd been introduced to some of the other Pendletons, Garth had stood apart. He obviously cared about them, but something kept him aloof, had made him a loner. The image caused a twist of pain in her. She understood about not fitting in.

"Hey, Erin," Garth called, his gaze full of questions. "You going to throw that ball today—or tomorrow?"

She shook off the disturbing feelings and took a deep breath. "Ready." She threw the pitch low, but they hit a grounder that rolled with the force Garth had put behind it.

Luke jumped up and down. "I did it! Look, I did it!"

"Hey, great pal," Garth said, smiling, "but we've

got a long way to go before celebrating." He put his hands around Luke's on the bat. "Okay, pitcher, another one over the plate."

Garth coached him. "Keep your eye on the ball."

It took four pitches before the ball met the bat with a resounding crack. Luke was beside himself with joy; Garth was grinning from ear to ear.

Pride and excitement kicked through Erin. "Great!" she yelled, and rushed to give Luke a hug. "You did great!" Erin could feel the pride bursting from his little body. She turned to Garth with extended hands, still excited, ready to embrace him.

Garth caught her in his arms and felt her stiffen, but he wasn't above using the situation to his advantage. The greedy devil inside him insisted on smelling her hair and memorizing how she felt pressed against him. It was an impersonal hug, he knew, and felt a burn of resentment. She'd been so excited about Luke's hit she would have hugged anyone. She wasn't clinging to him. She was allowing it. He slowly loosened his hold and let her move away. "Let's try that again."

Erin did a double take, her pulse racing a mile a minute. "Try what?"

"The pitching and the hitting." He cocked his head to one side. "What else?" he asked in a dangerous tone.

"Nothing," she insisted, striding back to her pitching location. Her eyes met Garth's and she felt breathless. With difficulty she forced herself to concentrate on the game. She managed to get the ball over the plate.

Luke hit the very next pitch. The ball slammed into Erin's chest.

"Oh, my God," she choked out, turning and clutching her left breast. Within seconds both Luke and Garth stood in front of her.

"You okay?" Garth asked.

"I'm sorry, Mom. I'm sorry. I didn't mean to hit you. Honest."

Erin heard the quavery note in her son's voice and bit the inside of her cheek to hide the pain. "Of course you didn't," she reassured him. "I stepped right in front of that ball." Keeping one hand over her chest, she reached down to hug him. "I'm just fine."

Luke looked at her skeptically. "I'm gonna get some ice," he announced. "That's what you always do for me." He ran toward the house.

"No. Luke," Erin called after him, but he was already gone. Wincing, she bit her lip and rocked from side to side.

"What hurts?" Garth asked.

Erin felt a flush of embarrassment. "Don't worry about it," she muttered, turning away.

He grabbed her arm. "Hey, wait." Hit hard by a mix of concern and impatience, he turned her around to face him. "Cut it out and tell me what's wrong."

She whispered a curse and tried to pull away,

but his hand didn't budge. She was so frustrated, she didn't know whether to laugh or to cry. This was ridiculous. "Can't you take a hint, Garth?"

He stopped, his gaze falling to her chest—and realization wiped the scowl from his face. "Oh."

"Yeah. Oh." She gave a little huff of indignation. "Maybe it'll swell."

The picture of masculine consternation, he released her, planted his hands on his hips, and looked down. "Well, hell, there's only one thing I can think of right now."

"What's that?"

"Want me to kiss it and make it better?"

# FOUR

An image rolled through Erin like sun-warmed honey of Garth with his avid mouth on her breasts, kissing and sucking. Dazed with desire, she forgot her pain.

Garth reached for her. "Are you okay?" he asked in a rough voice.

Erin shook her head in an indecisive circle. No. Yes. She took a deep breath to clear her mind, but his scent made her feel a little crazy.

His eyes darkened. "You want me to kiss you," he whispered. "You want my mouth on yours."

She couldn't deny it; she doubted she could even speak at the moment.

He leaned closer and put his mouth next to her ear. "You want my mouth on your breasts," he murmured.

Embarrassment made her stiffen and jerk her head

away. "I know I'm not well endowed," she said bluntly. "I'm sure you've noticed too. Let me go."

When she would have pulled away, Garth's hand tightened like a slipknot around her arm, and he lifted her chin with his thumb and forefinger. She glared at him.

"Such angry eyes. What would it take to get back that soft glazed look you wore just a minute ago?"

"Try letting me go."

His mouth quirked into a half grin. He shook his head knowingly. "You don't know much about men, Erin Lindsey."

"I never said I did," she retorted through gritted teeth.

"We were discussing my mouth on your breasts."

Erin felt a thrill of desire. She looked at the sky, seeking help. "I don't want to talk about this."

"Tough," he said calmly. "We can call it even, then. You're not getting what you want. If you press yourself against me, you'll see I'm not getting what I want either."

She sucked in a quick, shallow breath. There must be an appropriate response. Erin was sure there was. She just didn't know what it was.

He dropped her hand and in the same instant wrapped his arm around her waist. His free hand moved up her rib cage to rest below her breast. "Thinking about touching your nipples makes me wild."

Her mouth turned to dust.

His thumb rode a little higher, a breath shy of her aroused nipple. "I've wanted to touch you since I first saw you. I want to now. But I won't unless it's what you want too."

His gaze was hot and tender and melted her reserve. She closed her eyes, trying to find her inner sensibility. "Garth," she began in a shaky voice. "I—"

He moved his hand away, and she bit her lip.

"If you lean forward, just a little bit, I'll be there," he murmured. "Just a little bit, Erin," he coaxed. "Just for a minute."

She was caught in a swirl of should and want, right and wrong—but overriding everything was need. Where was her strength? Why did the choice seem beyond her? A second's more futile deliberation, and Erin swayed.

His warm hand gently cupped her breast. She felt his sigh against her cheek. Her own breath came in uneven spurts.

He palmed her nipple, and the sweetest ache coursed through her blood, shooting down her belly to her thighs. Irresistibly drawn, she looked up and saw the desire in his eyes. For her. It spun her head more effectively than a somersault. A rush of desperate need licked through her blood, and suddenly she had to have more of him.

It was reckless and crazy, but Erin was driven by what she'd never felt before . . . and by what she'd never seen on a man's face. Her hands closed around his neck, and she pulled his head down. The flash of surprise she saw crossing his face didn't daunt her. Erin pressed her mouth to his. He groaned and her nerves danced.

Sweeping his tongue over her lips, he tasted her as if he was a starving man and she was his first meal. He bit gently on her lower lip, then sucked it into his warm mouth, coaxing her to give him what he wanted.

He felt warm, masculine, and needy, so needy, it left her weak. Her knees went boneless, and when she stumbled, he caught her against him. His hand pushed against the small of her back so that she rocked against his hard arousal. His other hand threaded through her hair, tilting her head first this way, then that, kissing her with mind-blowing intensity.

Erin was overflowing with the desire to appease his hunger. With each flick of his tongue, each thrust of his body against hers, she felt herself climbing to a more heady plateau of excitement. The intensity of the emotions unleashed by the kiss frightened her.

With obvious reluctance he pulled his mouth from hers. "Luke'll be out here before we know it," he muttered against her mouth, breathing heavily, then kissing her again. "We'd better stop."

She gasped for air. "Luke."

Reality returned by slow degrees. Her skin still

tingled with arousal. Her mouth felt puffy and well kissed. Stifling a moan, Erin dropped her head to Garth's chest, feeling the thunder of his heartbeat. God, she was confused.

The sound of the screen door slamming made her straighten.

Garth allowed his hand to linger on her waist for a moment. "He's got a bag of ice. What are you gonna do?"

Still trying to collect herself, Erin watched Luke running toward them. "I'll tell him what a considerate boy he is, then I'll ask him if we can put the ice in lemonade."

Garth nodded, reluctant to let her move away. He liked his hands on her. He liked her hands on him. "Are you okay? I mean your"—he hesitated, then cursed his awkwardness—"your chest."

"Yes." She bit her lip.

He could almost see her building a wall of reserve. *The hell she would.* The devil nudged him. "But I never kissed it," he murmured, packing the statement with suggestion.

She pursed her lips in disapproval, but her eyes told a different story. "So you didn't."

Garth felt another curl of arousal deep in his gut. "Guess I'll have to take care of you some other time."

"We'll see."

Indeed he would see, Garth thought as Luke reached them.

After they shared lemonade and cookies, Luke ran out to catch the last few minutes of daylight play while Erin stacked the glasses and plates in the dishwasher.

Garth leaned against the counter, approving of the small room. With the copper cooking utensils hanging on the wall and the ruffled curtains at the window, it was feminine without being fussy. The refrigerator was covered with Luke's artwork. "Nice kitchen."

"Thanks. I'd like to do more, but if it's a choice between Luke, the horses, and decorating, I have to choose Luke first, the horses second." She faced him. "What about you?"

Garth shook his head. "I don't do much decorating."

"Oh, that's right," she said, gesturing for him to join her at the table. "You live with your brothers."

He took a seat, realizing this was the first time he'd been a guest in her house. "I live on the property, but I don't live in Daniel's house."

Erin looked confused. "Daniel's house?"

"My father died several years ago. Control of the land went to the eldest son, Daniel. Jarod and Troy live with Daniel. I live in a little cabin."

"And your mother?"

He felt a tug of sadness. "She died when I was twelve years old. My father changed, and by the time he remarried and my stepmother moved in, I was mad at God and everyone." He shook his head, remembering pain and overwhelming confusion. "I was hell to deal with. There wasn't a day that passed that my stepmother didn't tell me I was headed straight for hell if I didn't clean up my act." Feeling uncomfortable with his disclosure and Erin's sudden silence, Garth shrugged. "Sorry. I didn't mean to tell you more than you want to know." He started to get up.

Erin reached out to stop him, wrapping her small hand around his and tugging him back into his chair. "No. It's only that some of your past sounds a lot like mine."

He stared at her hand for a moment. So much compassion in such a small gesture. Why did his gut react when she touched him? He stroked her hand and looked at her. "You lost your parents too?"

"My mother died when I was eleven and my father also changed then." She looked down at the table-cloth. "He didn't remarry, though."

"When did he die?"

Her hand tightened. "Before Luke was born. It was an accident."

It still upset her. He could see it and feel it. "Must have been tough for you. My little sister was only four when Mom died. She stuttered for two years, and we were falling all over ourselves trying to help her."

"It was," she admitted. "Did having all those brothers get you through a little easier?"

Garth sighed, still stroking her fingers. "I don't know. I wasn't very good at talking things out back then. I'm still not good at it."

"A man of action?" Erin found herself smiling.

"Yeah. It's gotten me in trouble a few times."

She wondered if he was thinking about her father. She wished *she* wasn't. When had she sat across from a man at the kitchen table, sharing conversation while he played with her hands? Never. He seemed fascinated by her fingers. Her chest tightened with unfamiliar feelings. Arousal and something deeper, something more. She frowned.

"You've gotten quiet. Does my black soul terrify you?"

If anyone else had said that, she would have laughed. But he was serious. Puzzling over his question, Erin shook her head. "No. I wouldn't say it's your black soul."

His hands stopped their stroking, yet remained like a warm hug around hers. "But you're terrified."

"I don't know if *terrified* is the right word." When he remained silent, she rolled her eyes. "You're putting me on the spot. I don't exactly know what I feel."

He got the message. Lifting her palm to his lips, he watched her carefully. "What about when I do this?" He nuzzled her hand.

Her breath hitched. "I—uh, I—It's hard to breathe."

He kissed her fingers and leaned forward. "I want you, Erin Lindsey. And I intend to have you. If anyone's got a claim on you, better tell me now."

Her heart lurched. "No. I've never been married, but—"

"How did Luke—" Realization crossed his face. "Oh."

Feeling a sting of disappointment, Erin pulled her hand away. A lightning-quick jab of shame lit her temper. It brought back the way her father had reacted to what he called her "disgraceful behavior." "Yes, oh. I was seventeen when I got pregnant with Luke. My father died before he was born. It's been a tough road, but we've done okay. And as far as your intending to have me, don't get the wrong impression. Just because I made a mistake when I was a teenager doesn't mean I'm loose."

"I never said you were."

She immediately wished she hadn't confided in him. How had it happened? Where had her natural wariness gone? She'd never intended to reveal so much. Erin pushed back her chair and stood. "Your 'oh' said quite a bit."

Garth followed her to her feet, watching her carefully. He hadn't seen her this upset since the first time he'd met her. "You're reading too much into it."

"Right," she said in complete disbelief. "I'd appreciate it if you'd keep this confidential." She clenched her hands, and he watched her eyes widen with panic.

"God, if Luke suffers because I couldn't keep my mouth shut, I don't know—"

"Hell! Of course I'll keep it confidential." He wrapped his hand around her arm. When she tried to pull away from him, frustration grabbed at him. She didn't trust him, and for once it mattered. He refused to release her. "Dammit, Erin! Did you ever think I might be surprised? Did you ever think I'd be wondering what idiot would leave you once he had you? Did you ever think I'd wonder what kind of man wouldn't want Luke for a son?"

She took a deep breath and let it out slowly, her indignation deflating like a pricked balloon. "No."

"Then think again." He was out of his depth with her. He knew her volatile reaction must have something to do with her past. Something she wasn't telling him. "Babe, I don't know what's going on. But there's too much I don't know about you." He felt her stiffen again. "You say you're from out west. That could be anywhere from Texas to California." He watched her face, but she gave nothing away. "For that matter, it could mean Hawaii."

"That's right," she said in a voice colder than frost. "Now, if you will please let go of me."

He instantly dropped his hand. "Fine. But you're awful touchy about answering a few simple questions."

Her eyes flashed with anger. "I would think even you could understand someone's need for privacy."

*Direct hit.* Garth felt the impact. "Yeah, I understand," he said, a bitter taste filling his mouth. "But since we won't be playing Twenty Questions with each other, I guess you'll have to decide what's fact and fiction about me all on your own."

Erin heard the cynicism in his voice and instantly felt regret. She sighed. "I'm sorry. I shouldn't have said that. I, uh, guess I'm a little touchy. It's not your fault."

"A little?" He raised a dark eyebrow. "I'm glad you didn't have a knife in your hand."

Erin pressed her lips together, her normal good nature shot for the day. "You don't make it easy for me to apologize."

"Well, as you know, I'm not an easy man." His voice was low and rough. It seemed to ripple over her skin and stroke her with a hidden sultry nuance. "Let's make a deal."

She was wary. "What?"

"You don't make assumptions about me, and I won't make assumptions about you."

Erin swallowed. It was a reasonable suggestion. "Okay."

He pulled her toward the door as if he wanted to escape all that was unsettled and unknown between them. "Good. Let's go feed the ladies."

She allowed him to lead her along, but worried. At first she'd worried that Garth was a physical threat to her. Now she *knew* he was. He made her sizzle. He made her vulnerable. But what worried her more was the dangerous way he managed to make her open up, and there were things she could never tell him. Never. If he learned the truth, it could be disastrous for Luke, for her, for everyone.

She needed to pull back.


Three days later Erin continued to tell herself that backing away from Garth was the right thing to do, but he didn't make it easy. Even though he found two teenagers to take over most of the barn work, he still checked on her every night. She came to the disquieting conclusion that he was ready and willing to follow her down the hall to her bedroom any time she even hinted at it.

The notion provoked hours of excruciating excitement. If she ever made love with Garth Pendleton, would she do something crazy and embarrassing like freeze or faint? He was too big, too experienced, too sexy.

Involvement between them would only end with someone getting hurt, most likely her, maybe Luke. Garth could brush off his losses, she rationalized. He was a loner. Besides, anything that happened between them would probably hold more significance to her. He seemed the kind of man who'd taught himself to keep his emotions in check.

Deep down, though, her reasoning didn't ring true. She felt as if she were walking in the dark when it came to Garth: disoriented because he was beyond her limited experience, thrilled because he wanted her. The dear Lord knew she wanted him.

She did her best to put him out of her mind, focusing on her mares. After a successful morning spent coaxing a three-year-old into accepting a transition in her gaits, Erin double-checked the fences.

For grazing purposes she'd changed pastures a few days before after checking the fences. Everything looked fine until she walked to the west pasture. All the mares were inside the fence. Except one.

Erin's adrenaline pumped into overdrive when she saw her prize temperamental mare whinnying at the top of her lungs. Bright sunlight reflected off the sheen of sweat and blood on her flank.

Her heart sank. "Oh, God." The fence was broken open just enough to get out but not enough for Rapunzel to get back in. The agitated mare stood next to the water trough. Erin guessed she'd probably gotten overheated and drunk too much water too fast. For a mare in foal, that could easily mean colic. Another whinney broke the afternoon quiet.

Erin felt the edge of panic. She fought it down. The horse was panicked enough; she had to keep her head. Her feet started moving as she murmured a litany of pleading prayers under her breath.

She managed to transfer the horses to another pasture, then kicked out part of the fence. Her composure was hanging by a thread. How had it happened?

When? The questions flew through her mind at the same time she worried that Rapunzel was headed for shock.

Keeping her voice low and soothing, Erin guided the horse through the broken fence and back to the barn. She spent the next hour walking Rapunzel, but it seemed the mare grew more lethargic. Noticing that the mare felt clammy, Erin checked her gums.

"Damn." Erin ran to the phone and called the vet. When the secretary said he wouldn't make it until later that night, Erin nearly wept. She fought back the fear that she could lose both Rapunzel and her foal. Then she acted on instinct. She called Garth, but there was no answer, so she dialed an alternate number he'd given her.

"Pendleton's," the deep voice said.

Erin immediately knew it wasn't Garth. "I need to speak to Garth." She heard her own shaky voice and tried to make it firm as she added, "Please."

A long pause followed. "Last I saw him, he was out helping Daniel. But I'm not sure where—"

"Could you tell him Erin Lindsey called?" She needed to get off the phone, get herself together so that she could help Rapunzel. "I'm having a problem with one of my mares, and the vet can't come and—"

"Hold on. Let me get this straight."

"No. I don't have time. I've got a mare in foal going into shock." She took a quick breath. "Just tell Garth I called. Please." Then she hung up and ran back outside and tried not to feel so totally alone. There had been other times she'd felt alone like this. When she'd received the news that her father had died. When Luke had been delirious with fever in the middle of the night. Scared and utterly, completely alone.

She'd made it through those times, Erin reminded herself. She'd make it again. And damned if Rapunzel and her baby wouldn't make it too.

"Garth! Hey, Garth!"

Garth looked up from the fence he was helping Daniel mend to see Troy running across the field. His young brother worked hard at keeping his cool, so Garth figured something exciting must have happened.

By the time Troy reached Daniel and Garth, he was out of breath. "Erin—" He took a breath.

Garth shot up straight, letting Daniel take the weight of the fence post. "Erin. What's wrong? Did something happen to Luke?"

Troy held up a hand, shaking his head. "No. It's one of her mares. She said something about the horse going into shock and she couldn't get the vet. I tried to get her to tell me more, but she hung up on me."

Garth relaxed marginally at the same time that he wondered which mare had the problem. "When did she call?"

"Just now. I ran right over."

Garth nodded and turned to Daniel. "It sounds like she's in trouble. You think you can handle this while I go?" He was already handing his tool belt to Troy.

"You've been spending a lot of time over there lately."

Garth chafed at the undertone he heard in Daniel's voice. In the last couple of weeks his oldest brother, usually calm and even-tempered, had exhibited a mean streak that would try the patience of Job. "Erin's a neighbor. She doesn't have any family. I told you all that."

Daniel rubbed the back of his hand against his cheek. "It doesn't hurt that she's got the kind of horse farm you'd trade your Harley and every last dime for."

"Maybe. I've made no secret of what I want."

Daniel frowned. "You don't understand. We need to add something to the farm that will show a return faster than horses would."

Garth brushed the excess dirt off his hands. "I understand just fine, Daniel. You've got to do what you need to do. And I've gotta do what I need to do."

He muttered "Thanks" to Troy, then started walking away.

"Like the time you took off for Denver."

The statement stopped him cold. He took a deep

breath. Garth knew Daniel had been disappointed when he'd gone out west for nine months instead of finishing college. Daniel didn't know the whole story, though, he assured himself. His family knew about the girl who'd dumped him and they knew something bad had happened in Denver. Daniel, Carly, and Troy had even said that they'd be willing to listen if Garth wanted to talk, but he hadn't, so no one in his family knew for certain what had brought him back from Denver.

He gritted his teeth. It was a low blow for Daniel to bring it up. Garth reined in his irritation and refused to take the bait. Why was Daniel walking around in a perpetual foul mood, begging for a fight? The hell with a question like that now. He had to get to Erin.

# FIVE

Garth found Erin in the barn, murmuring soothingly to the distressed mare. Rapunzel was quiet—and down on her side in the hay. It didn't look good. "Did you get the vet?"

Startled, Erin whipped around, clutching her shirt. She took a deep breath and sagged. "You scared me to death. Don't you ever make any noise when you walk?"

He shrugged, coming closer, seeing the nerves in her tight expression, the wilting ribbon around her ponytail, and the determination in her raised chin. He jammed his hands in his pockets to keep from taking her into his arms. "Guess not."

"Try stomping next time."

In spite of the dire circumstances, he felt a lick of amusement. The lady got cranky when she was nervous. He'd have to remember that. So much for his fantasy that she'd meet him with open arms. "Did you call Art Goldman?"

Erin shook her head, her attention back on Rapunzel. "Who is he?"

"Retired vet. He'll come." He started to head out of the barn.

"Garth."

He stopped and turned, waiting expectantly.

Erin looked up at him, her eyes full of an expression that grabbed at his heart and gently squeezed. "Thank you for coming."

He wanted to kiss her. "No problem," he said instead. "Just being—"

"Neighborly," Erin finished for him.

He thought about correcting her, but she'd backed off, and he'd been cooling his heels for the last few days, learning a lesson about moving too fast. "Yeah, right. Neighborly." Then he made a promise to himself: He'd have this neighbor in his bed by Thanksgiving.

Hours later, after Dr. Goldman had treated Rapunzel and it looked as if the mare would make it, Erin grilled sandwiches and heated soup for a late dinner. She looked at the clock and made a face. It was Luke's bedtime.

"Luke," she yelled out the kitchen window. "Time for dinner, sweetie."

She flipped the sandwiches onto plates and caught

a whiff of the odor the day had left her with. "I smell like a horse," she muttered.

"What did you say?" Garth asked from behind her.

Erin felt a quick flush of heat, wishing she looked better, smelled sweeter. "Nothing. Sandwiches and soup are ready."

"Fine."

"I don't have any beer," she went on, putting the food on the table. "It's either Rock-A-Dile-red Kool-Aid, Coke, or milk." She looked up.

He hitched his thumbs into his pockets and leaned back against the counter, shifting his hips slightly. Warm, mussed, and sexy, he reminded her of a stud. In spite of herself, Erin noticed and felt a potent, elemental awareness of him. She had a strong urge to burrow her face into his neck and press herself to him to feel his muscled chest against her breasts and his hard thighs between hers. She'd like to . . . but she wouldn't. Erin forced her gaze up to his face.

"I'll take milk." His lips quirked into a half grin. "Rock-A-Dile red? What happened to plain ol' cherry?"

"Marketing?" Erin pulled the jar of pickles from the refrigerator and fashioned a face out of two round slices for eyes and a slice of banana for a mouth. She shuddered at the flavor combination.

"Hey, Mom, I found a rotten egg!" Luke called, running in. "I already washed my hands," he said before she could ask. "Did you fix me a clown face?"

"Of course." She kissed his cheek and nudged him toward the table. "What'd you do with the rotten egg?"

"Put it in the trash like you told me I should." He frowned at the milk on his place mat. "How come I don't get Rock-A-Dile-red Kool-Aid?"

She caught Garth's knowing glance and smiled. "It's too late at night. If you drink Kool-Aid too late, you'll turn into a crocodile." Which wasn't far from the truth. The sugar would make him bounce off the walls. Erin scooted into her chair. "Then I wouldn't have the best little boy in the world. How horrible."

Luke rolled his eyes. "M-o-o-o-m." But he giggled when she poked his ribs.

Garth watched them, feeling a powerful yearning. Erin was tired and spent. He could tell by the shadows under her eyes. But she still took the time to fix a clown face and tickle her son out of his disappointment. His respect and admiration for her had grown, too, when he'd seen how she handled the emergency with Rapunzel. There was a strong inner core underneath the delicate feminine exterior. The knowledge made her more attractive to him than ever.

"I don't want to go to bed right after dinner. I want to stay up and make sure Rapunzel's okay."

Erin's expression softened. "I know it makes Rapunzel happy that you're so concerned about her, but Dr. Goldman said she and her baby are going to be just fine. You have to go to school tomorrow, so you need your sleep."

Luke clearly didn't agree. "Well, you need your sleep too." His sandwich demolished, he toyed with his soup and yawned.

Erin smiled. "I'll try to catch a nap tomorrow sometime."

"How come you get to stay up and I don't?"

Garth expected another patient explanation until he looked at Erin's face.

"Because I'm bigger than you are," she said in a gentle, but no-nonsense tone. "Now, go say good night to Rapunzel. Five minutes till bedtime."

Luke started to protest. "But Mom—"

"Four minutes and fifty-eight seconds."

The little boy stood quickly. "Okay, but can Garth help put me to bed?"

She paused, glancing at Garth. "W-e-l-l. He probably needs to get back to his—"

"I'd like that, Luke." He held his breath, sensing her indecision.

"Okay. Hurry, honey." After Luke skipped out of the room, Erin turned back to Garth. "I don't want you to feel obligated to—"

"I don't," he interjected, feeling oddly that he'd just won a significant victory. "I might as well since I'll be staying in your barn tonight."

Erin looked confused. "You don't have to do that. I'd already planned to put a cot out there for myself."

He took his dishes to the counter and prepared for an argument. She hadn't failed him yet. "I'll take the cot. You can catch your sleep in your own bed."

"I can't let you do that. Rapunzel's my horse, my responsibility."

"I won't complain if you want to join me. Might be kinda tough with that little cot, though." His voice deepened. "You'd probably have to lie on top of me."

Erin suddenly felt hotter than a branding iron. The vivid image of being on top of Garth sent her hormones surging to sensitive points throughout her body. Embarrassed, Erin bit her lip and looked down at the table. "That isn't what I meant, and you know it."

"I'm staying the night in the barn. The vet said someone needed to check on Rapunzel."

"You're being pushy."

"And you're arguing."

Erin opened her mouth to make another point, then closed it. She looked at him. He was dirty, tired, and insistent. No other man had ever been more attractive to her. Watching Garth today while he helped Dr. Goldman, encouraged her, and comforted Luke had caused something inside her to shift. A few more bricks had been knocked out of her protective wall. The situation had been dire, and he'd come through for her. She wouldn't be able to look at him in the same distant way again.

She shifted uncomfortably. She still didn't want

him staying overnight—even in the barn. "Tell me one good reason why you should stay up with *my* mare instead of me."

He crossed his arms over his muscled chest and leaned forward, his lips suddenly far too close. Yet too far away. His eyes were violet lodestones, searing her with their intensity, his body heat cranking up her internal temperature. "Because I'm bigger than you are."

Erin fell asleep the moment her head hit the pillow, thinking she could have slept until January. Sometime after midnight, though, she woke. She might have gone back to sleep if she hadn't started thinking. Thoughts of Rapunzel, Luke, and Garth poked at her, making rest impossible. The covers on her bed were a twisted mess; she got up and pulled on a pair of jeans and socks.

She took a few restless turns around the house, checked on Luke, and drank a glass of water. Then she gave up and decided to look in on Rapunzel— just for a minute, she told herself as she shoved her arms into a jacket. She'd be in and out so quickly, she wouldn't wake Garth.

Armed with a flashlight, Erin made her way to the barn, only tripping once. She carefully, quietly cracked the door open a sliver, clicked off the flashlight, and went in. Erin sucked in a quick breath at the absolute blackness. She felt her way along the wall, her steps quiet.

"You don't have to worry about waking me up, Erin," Garth said right next to her ear. "I'm not—"

"Dammit Garth! I told you to stomp. Stomp," she hissed, whipping around to face him.

He steadied her shoulders. "Sorry." She heard a note of amusement in his voice. He coughed. "Forgot."

"Right," she said darkly. "Since you're awake, can I turn on the light?"

He paused a half second. "Yeah, but—"

Erin found the wall switch and clicked it—and for the life of her, wished she'd left it off. Garth Pendleton stood in front of her in full male glory. Gloriously nude. She closed her eyes, but not before the sight of his body branded itself on her conscious, subconscious, unconscious. She suspected she'd need years of therapy to forget it.

His broad, powerful shoulders and sinewy arms were up to providing protection from danger or comfort for a woman in a long, dark, lonely night. And God knows she'd had her share of lonely nights. His muscular chest with silky-looking black hair that narrowed into a slim stream down the front of his flat abdomen to cup his masculinity was enough to make a woman moan. It was all too easy to imagine being the woman beneath his hands and body. It was all too easy to imagine being the woman to touch him and bring a moan from his mouth. Her blood quickened through her veins at an alarming rate.

Erin swallowed hard, but her mind went on, reminding her of his strong thighs lightly dusted with dark hair, making her think of being the one trapped beneath him.

"Am I that ugly?"

Erin's eyes popped open and she immediately fixed them on the ceiling. "You could have warned me."

"I tried, but you turned on the light before—"

"Okay. Okay. Do you think you could pull on some clothes?"

"Yeah, give me a minute."

Erin heard him turn, then the rustle of denim against flesh. A wild, impudent impulse nudged her to take a peak at his backside, but she restrained herself. She heard the scrape of a zipper. Why did every little sound seem like it was in stereo? Why did she feel so breathless?

"I'm decent," he told her.

Erin looked at him and begged to differ. He wore the jeans. His hair was irresistibly tousled, his jaw marked with a trace of stubble, and his gorgeous bare chest had her flexing her fingers like a cat flexing her claws on a satin pillow. He absently squeezed his left shoulder with his right hand. She wondered if it hurt. "I, uh. I woke up and couldn't go back to sleep, so I thought I'd check on Rapunzel." She walked over closer to the stall.

"She's fine." He moved closer, and they both looked at the sleeping mare.

"Well," Erin said, pushing her hair behind her ear. "Looks like everything's fine out here. Are you okay? Do you need another blanket?"

Garth shook his head, then rubbed his shoulder again. "No, I don't like too many covers at night. Makes me feel trapped. That's why I wasn't dressed when you came in."

Erin cleared her throat. "Right."

"How about you?"

Her eyes widened. "Are you talking about covers or—or—sleep wear?"

He gave her a lazy grin. "Either."

This discussion was ridiculous. But then many discussions begun in the middle of the night were ridiculous. "I guess I'm just the opposite. Lots of covers make me feel secure."

Garth thought Erin wouldn't need blankets to make her secure if she spent the night with him. He'd do it with his body. He wondered if she would have admitted wanting security in the light of day, or if only the hushed darkness allowed her to admit it. He wondered many things about Erin—what her bare skin felt like, how she liked to be held, what her secrets were—and if she ever wanted him half as much as he wanted her.

"You're rubbing your shoulder," Erin said. "Did you hurt it?"

Garth glanced down at his hand on his shoulder and felt surprised. He shook his head. "I didn't notice."

Erin slanted her head in skepticism. "If you're rubbing it, you must have noticed it." She held his gaze for a moment, her eyes shimmering with uncertainty, then a flash of compassion. Then she sighed in resignation. "Would you like me to rub it for you?"

He instantly felt a twist of excitement. The thought of her hands on him made him hot. He caught the concerned expression on her face. *She's not offering this for foreplay, idiot.* Erin was offering because she was a caring woman. Surprisingly the notion didn't diminish his arousal; it turned him on more.

He ought to say no thanks. "Yeah. That'd be nice. You want me to sit?" He walked swiftly to the cot before she changed her mind.

"I guess." Erin followed, wondering if she'd lost her mind. It was this damned nurturing gene she had. She hated seeing someone hurt, especially if she cared about that someone. And though it didn't please her, she knew she cared more than she wanted to about the sexy tomcat in her barn.

She put the flashlight down. The soft light of the overhead bulb lent a sheen to his smoothly muscled skin. She lifted her hands and hesitated, then took a deep breath. She'd almost swear he was holding his breath too.

Slowly Erin reached out and touched his shoulder. His warmth surprised her. "Your shoulder's tight."

He nodded, rotating it a bit beneath her hands. After a moment a long breath eased out of him and he seemed to relax.

"You've got good hands," he said, his voice low and raspy. Her shadow danced on the wall. He watched it for a few minutes, then closed his eyes, and his sense of her became sharper.

He felt her breath on the back of his neck and the rhythmical massage of her fingers. The sleeve of her jean jacket rubbed against him every now and then. Gentle, yet firm, she kneaded his shoulder until the soreness was gone. She widened her attention to his other shoulder and neck; her long, smooth strokes worked magic until his upper body was completely relaxed. And his lower body was completely tense.

Garth inhaled her clean, feminine scent—a heady combination of sleep, flowers, and soft womanliness. Wanting it to permeate, he breathed in more strongly and caught a whiff of his own odor. He laughed gruffly.

"What?"

"I smell like a horse."

"Hmmm."

The sound came out like a lazy murmur of amusement. He couldn't see her face, but he'd bet she was smiling. "What does 'Hmmm' mean?"

She ran her fingers up under the edge of his hair,

and a shiver of pleasure ran down his back. "I said the same thing about myself earlier this evening."

"You smell great now. What are you wearing?"

She shrugged. "Soap and me."

He turned to look at her. "Must be the 'me' part that got my attention."

Her gaze darkened. Garth watched uncertainty creep in. She started to pull her hands away. "I guess it's time—"

He caught her hands and pressed them against his mouth, closing his eyes for a second at the texture of her skin. "Don't stop. Not yet."

A delicious weakness spread through her. Erin locked her knees to keep from pitching forward into his arms. His mouth against her skin was sensual soft. She couldn't have pulled away for a million dollars.

He looked up and tugged her closer. "Erin, why'd you come out here tonight?"

She couldn't tell if he was a little angry or a little aroused. She decided the two together usually equaled frustrated. Mixed feelings surged through her. She tried to maintain some reason. "You know why. To check on Rapunzel."

He caught one of her fingers between his teeth, then drew it into his mouth. Her breasts grew tight. Erin closed her eyes. "Garth," she managed to say.

He gradually released her finger and kissed it. "Just to check on Rapunzel."

"I couldn't sleep."

"And you weren't thinking about me." His voice vibrated against her skin.

Sensual panic sliced through her. She swallowed. "Garth. Don't."

"Don't what, baby?" He gave a quick tug and pulled her off balance, sending her falling against him. He turned her onto the cot.

Her heart pounded in her throat. Flat on her back now with him leaning over her, she stared up at him. He was more dark than light, both shadow and substance, threat and comfort. A fast and furious desire slammed through her.

"Don't make me say it out loud," she whispered desperately.

Garth took a long pull of air. For an instant he saw the panic on her face and felt like a madman ravaging a princess. Then he looked closer and saw something else: arousal, strong and overwhelming. The realization scraped at his thin layer of restraint.

"Say what?" He sifted his fingers through her silky hair. She arched her neck against his hand in a telling, involuntary movement.

"Say that you weren't thinking about me instead of sleeping? Is that right, lady?" He leaned forward and watched her eyes dilate as he edged closer and closer. "Say that you're a little more than curious about the Pendleton Devil. Huh?"

He nuzzled her jaw and heard her audible swallow.

"Pendleton—" She swallowed again. "Pendleton Devil?"

Garth shifted away, reading the curiosity on her face. "Yeah. You haven't heard?"

Erin shook her head. "No."

Feeling predatory, Garth smiled. "It's my nickname."

"I guess I can see why," she muttered, looking away.

He felt his smile fall. He wanted her trust, damn it. It made little sense, but despite his reputation, he wanted her to trust him. He cupped her chin to bring her attention back to him. "Does it scare you?"

"The nickname . . . doesn't."

He narrowed his eyes and looked at her carefully, seeing the flush of arousal still on her face. Her jacket had slid open to reveal the hardened tips of her nipples against her white nightshirt.

"But the way you want me does, doesn't it?" He skimmed his hand down her chest to where her heart hammered. A soft gasp escaped her lips. "Your little heart's racing, Erin." He made his tone deliberately suggestive, a bit goading. He wanted something from her. He wanted a confession.

He barely brushed his fingers across her breasts and saw her fight to keep from pushing against him. A coil of heat settled low in his loins. "Feels so good, it almost hurts, doesn't it?"

He skimmed his hand down to her gently curved

abdomen. "C'mon, sweet Erin. I want to hear it." His hand moved lower, cupping the source of her pleasure. "I want to hear," he said roughly as he lowered his head, "that you want me half as much as I want you."

# SIX

It was too much. He was too much. His body pressed against hers, his hand between her legs, his eyes glowing with arousal, and his voice—heaven help her, if he'd kept his mouth shut, she might have stood a chance.

Erin struggled for breath. Hot and cold sensations shivered and bucked along her nerve endings from head to toe. She finally managed a shaky breath of air, but it was more of a sob.

He rubbed his hand against her again, making her melt and moisten. Her thoughts scandalous, her body primed, she was a mass of contradictions. She wished they were naked so that she could feel every inch of him and he could make love to her.

She shut her eyes when she saw him lower his head. His warm breath fanned across her face. He slid his mouth against hers, then swirled his tongue over her lips.

"Tell me," he whispered, then tasted her again, "what do you feel?"

She felt like a sensual volcano about to erupt. The strength of her hunger for him was both shocking and profound. It was like nothing she'd ever experienced.

Gasping, she jerked her head to the side, silently pleading for deliverence. His hot mouth found her neck. "Oh, God." She swallowed. "I feel—" she broke off, shaking her head—"too much." Erin opened her eyes. "Too much," she repeated helplessly.

Garth saw the desire. He saw the fear. But he felt her vulnerability, her susceptibility to him, and he experienced something new. Never in the grip of lust with an aroused woman in his arms had he experienced compassion.

He moved his hand away from the warmth between her thighs, noting the shudder that racked her. He continued up to thread his fingers through her hair to soothe her. Then he touched her moistened lips with his thumb. "Poor baby. All turned on and don't know what to do about it. It's been a long time, hasn't it?"

Feeling self-conscious, she stiffened.

"It's okay," he said quickly. "I can tell . . ." His voice trailed off when he saw the frown on her face.

Erin turned her head away from him. "I know you're more experienced than I am, but you don't have to rub it in. My past really isn't any of your business."

*None of his business.* The words vibrated unpleasant-
ly. She was obviously sensitive about her experience
or, rather, her lack of it, but her desire for privacy
roused something dark and primal in Garth. Something he couldn't explain to himself, let alone to Erin.
He took her mouth, no hesitation, no apologies. It
was a no-frills, I'm-gonna-have-you kiss. By the time
he stopped, they were both breathing hard, and her
eyes were glazed.

"If I want to know something about your past, it's
because I want to make sure making love will be as
good for you as it is for me." His voice deepened.
"Everything about you is my business, Erin. Everything. Since I'm gonna be the next man to make love
to you."

Angry, yet still aroused, she swallowed hard. "Okay!
One man."

Garth stopped, staring at her. He hadn't expected
that. Two, maybe three. But Erin was too pretty
to have gotten involved only once and long ago.

"Am I supposed to tell you how many times, now?"
Her voice trembled with anger. "Three. Two times in
the barn and once in the backseat."

Garth felt a twinge of regret. He could tell it was
a painful subject. "Erin—"

"No. Let me finish. I want you to know what I
remember about it. He held me and told me that he
loved me, and I was so lonely and stupid that I would
have done anything to hear it. The best word I can

use to describe those experiences was *fast*." He saw the hurt shimmering in her eyes and felt like a heel.

"Turnabout's fair play, Garth. How many women?" Her voice deepened in accusation. "Can you count that high?"

A fast, sharp pain took his breath. "You've got good aim. You're right. I couldn't count them all. There was a time when I went through women like a stud goes through mares. But I protected myself and them, if that's what you're worried about." He shifted so that he could better see her face. "If you're asking what I remember about all those women—"

"No." Erin cringed, thinking better of asking her questions. She really didn't want to know about his other experiences. The discussion turned her stomach. When he opened his mouth again, she shook her head.

Garth placed his fingers over her lips. "If you want to know what I remember about all those women, I can't help you out," he said, his voice full of frustration. "I can't remember a damn thing when I'm with you."

Speechless, she blinked, struggling to comprehend him. An unbidden warmth spread through her. His expression was hard, but she suspected all that hardness hid a deep vulnerability. She softened at the thought. He shifted, and the light played on his shoulder, revealing a jagged scar. Her gaze caught on it, and her heart took a dip. An uneasy suspicion thudded through her. "Your scar. It must have hurt when it happened."

"Yeah." The word was reluctantly drawn from him.

"Is that what makes your shoulder hurt?"

His mouth tightened. "I guess."

"How long—" Erin swallowed. "How long have you had it?" she whispered.

"Seven years."

It hit her like the bullet that must have hit him. She hadn't known he'd been shot. Her throat squeezed into a tight knot, and she felt the sting of tears. "I'm sorry. God, I'm sorry." Erin curled herself into him.

Surprised, Garth wrapped his arms around her and cuddled her. He was amazed. She caught him completely off guard. Her tenderness tugged at his heart so hard, it hurt. He couldn't think of anything to say. He couldn't possibly tell her how he'd gotten the wound. She wouldn't understand that he'd been forced to kill a man. Sometimes he still didn't understand it.

The wetness of her tears on his neck made him ache. He tilted her head and looked into her anguished eyes. And because there weren't any words, he kissed her.

He tasted her gently, sipping at her lips, then gained entry with his tongue into her sweetness. He caught her sigh and withstood the urge to plunder until she sucked his tongue in invitation. His body instantly tightened, and a rough growl escaped his throat.

Garth molded his hand around her jaw and cheeks, massaging to open her mouth further for his exploration. Her hands slid restlessly to his bare shoulders and squeezed. He felt the hint of her nipples, muffled by the covering of her shirt brushing against his chest. It was too hot for clothes.

Their mouths made breathless sucking noises of need. Sliding his hand down to her shirt, he undid the buttons, then brushed the shirt aside and rubbed his bare chest against her hardened nipples. He let out a groan of need. "I've wanted to do this since the first time I saw you."

Caught in the mesmerizing spell of their passion, Erin's head was spinning. He slid his knee between her legs, and her heart seemed to stop. Reluctantly releasing her mouth, he kissed his way down her throat and chin, leaving her skin tingling.

He rested his chin on her ribs and looked at her breasts as if he were going to ravish her. Excitement quivered through her. Her small movement captured all his attention. He shifted his gaze and stared at her with hot, violet eyes. Erin's mouth went dry as dust.

"I'm gonna show you what I think of your body, Erin Lindsey. After I finish, there'll be no misunderstanding me."

Watching her carefully, he lowered his warm mouth to the underside of her breast. Her nipples peaked in the cool air, begging for his attention, but Garth was taking his time. She muffled a tiny sound of frustration and closed her eyes.

He pulled his mouth away, and she almost cried out. "Open your eyes, baby. I want you to watch." His voice deepened to black velvet. "And I want to watch you."

Her gaze met his. The wanting, the incredible wanting grew stronger. "I want you so much, I hurt," she whispered.

His eyes darkened into pools of turbulent passion, and he pressed his thumb against her lower lip. "Waiting makes it better."

Holding her gaze, he kissed ever-smaller circles around her aching breasts. It was the most erotic experience of her life watching him indulge his hunger for her, first with his lips, then with his tongue. A flush of heat suffused her inside and out.

Closer and closer he moved to her stiff, sensitized nipples. Erin held her breath. Every inch of her body was tensed and waiting. He was almost there.

He paused just a second longer, then flicked his tongue lazily over her nipple. She jerked. A surge of sensation shot through her.

Covering her aureole, he drew it deep into his mouth. Erin felt the tug low in her abdomen. She cried out, arching against him.

He pulled back and muttered roughly, "It's okay, baby."

He switched his avid mouth to her other nipple at the same time Erin felt his hand release the button to her jeans. An alarm went off in her head. She should stop him, now, before they went too far. She opened her mouth, but ended up gasping for air.

His fingers slid under the edge of her panties.

A dangerous thrill raced through her. It was irresistible, but she *needed* to resist it. A primitive instinct warned that she might end up losing. "Garth," she managed to say.

He nibbled on her breasts and slipped his fingers closer to her warmth. "What?"

She swallowed hard. "We need to—" Her voice broke off when he found the most sensitive point in her body. She sucked in a desperate breath. "Stop. Please, stop."

He paused and lifted his head to look at her face. "Why?"

Distressed, Erin shook her head, not knowing how to explain it. "I'm not ready."

He made a rough sound of disbelief. "Baby, you're about as ready as a woman gets. You're wet and hot, and it probably wouldn't take me but a minute—"

She put her hands around his wrist. "That's not what I meant. I'm not ready for *you*."

He looked at her for a long, tense moment. Then,

giving a heavy sigh, he removed his hands from her, stood, and swung his leg over the cot. She immediately missed his warmth as he walked away.

Erin could sense his frustration. He threaded his hand through his hair and leaned over Rapunzel's stall, staring into nothing.

She grimaced. What a mess. She buttoned her shirt and slowly rose from the cot. He probably thought she was a tease. The least she could do was try to explain.

She edged closer to him. "I'm sorry."

"Forget it."

Her body was still humming. Erin gave a short, self-deprecating laugh. "Not likely."

When he didn't respond, she tentatively touched his shoulder.

Garth flinched and turned on her, quick as a snake. "Leave it alone. Go back to bed where you belong."

Pulling on her courage, she lifted her chin. "I said I'm sorry and I meant it. It's been a long time for me, Garth, and you're overwhelming." She held out her hands in front of his face. "Look at my hands. They're still shaking."

He looked at her hands, then met her gaze for a hot, potent second. "You'll excuse me if I don't sympathize, since my body probably won't cool down till Christmas."

"I'm sorry."

"So, what are you gonna do about it?"

She felt a kick deep in her stomach. "Don't ask me that." She closed her eyes for an anguish-filled moment. "I don't know. Maybe being in a barn brought back some memories. Maybe I'm worried about getting pregnant."

"I would protect you."

Erin shook her head and laid her cards on the table. "Yes, you would. Physically. But what about emotionally?"

The question took the edge off his anger. He looked at her warily. "What do you mean?"

"I mean what kind of man are you really? Underneath the Pendleton Devil, what kind of man are you?"

Garth shrugged. She was leading him into uncharted territory. "What you see is what you get. I'm no prince."

"I'm not sure you're right about that." With a heavy sigh Erin brushed her mussed hair back from her face, and he had to resist the urge to do it for her. He tightened his grip on the stall door. "I want to know who you are on the inside, Garth Pendleton."

She met his gaze with strong, womanly determination. He felt his heartbeat pick up. Hell. The woman was alternately arousing him and scaring him. "You're crazy."

"Probably," she said, but her eyes were still glowing with the kind of look that got close to something gushy and sentimental.

"I'm not making any promises," he said swiftly.

The glow went out. She gave a forced smile. "That's okay. I'm used to men who either don't make promises or don't keep them." She turned toward the door. "G'night, Garth."

He tried. He really tried to let her go. But his heart twisted so hard, he felt like he was on a rack. Wrenching away from the stall door, he took two steps, jerked her around, and kissed her. The heat inside him rose instantly. She responded, and he wanted her so badly, he thought he'd die of it.

"I'm a rotten man, Erin," he warned her harshly. "Rotten to the core." Garth knew any favors he'd done for Erin were for the selfish purpose of getting into her bed. He kissed her soft mouth again. "There's not an ounce of goodness in me. I swear."

She stared at him and shook her head. Slowly, she ran her hands up his neck to his cheeks. "You're lying. If you weren't good, you wouldn't warn me." She rose up on tiptoe, then rocked his foundations by looking him straight in the eye and saying, "You've warned me. Now let me find out for myself."

The next evening after dinner Erin watched Garth teach Luke karate. This was the first time Luke hadn't felt self-conscious about being watched—which Erin took as a sign that he was growing in self-confidence. So she watched. Not with an idle every-now-and-then glance through the window. She left the dishes in the sink, sat down in one of the rockers on the porch, and shamelessly watched every move they made.

She noticed the way Garth steadied Luke when his balance was off. She noticed the way he patted Luke on the shoulder and encouraged him. She also noticed the way Luke was doing his very best to please Garth.

The scene reminded her of the riding instructor long ago who'd helped her overcome her fear of jumping. She'd been a tense and resistant pupil, but he must have seen a glimmer of potential in her. That was when her love for horses had begun. That instructor probably had no idea how much his extra effort had meant to her.

She wondered if anyone had ever expressed belief in Garth's potential. She thought not and felt awful pain.

They were doing some kind of kicks. Garth's movements were smooth, fluid. Erin shifted in her seat. The man was sensual even when executing a kick. She wondered if martial arts made his awareness of his body more acute. Memories of last night came to mind, and she felt an instant infusion of heat. He wasn't the kind of man who would make a woman guess what pleased him. He'd be able to tell her in breath-robbing terms.

Despite the cooling temperatures Erin lifted her hair off the back of her neck to fan her hot skin.

At that moment Garth glanced up and met her gaze.

She felt caught.

Her cheeks were flushed, she knew, because of what she'd been thinking.

His lips tilted into a knowing grin that sent a thrill of anticipation running through her. He murmured something to Luke, then nudged her son toward the porch.

"Hey, Mom, look at this neat kick Garth taught me." Luke gave a quick, awkward replica of Garth's, but he managed to stay on his feet.

"Great job!" Erin said. "I'm impressed." And she was. With both of them.

Luke's chest puffed out. "Wait'll you hear my *kyop*. Garth says I could probably scare a dead person." He bowed respectfully, then as he jerked into fighting stance, he let out a bloodcurdling yell.

Erin jumped. She watched, confused, as Garth nodded in approval. "What do you call that?"

"It's a *kyop*, Mom. It's one of the first important self-defense techniques," Luke said importantly. "And I'm gonna practice every morning and every night." Then, exhibiting the attention span of a typical six-year-old, he switched the subject. "Can I watch cartoons before I go to bed?"

"Please," Erin reminded him, her ears still ringing.

"Please," he said. He stunned her by turning to Garth and hugging him. The affectionate gesture apparently took Garth by surprise, too, but he bent over and wrapped his arms around Luke.

"Thanks, Mr. Pendleton. See ya tomorrow." Then her little heartthrob was running straight for the television.

Erin felt a lump in her throat and watched Garth, wondering if he'd been similarly affected. "Rotten to the core, huh?" she asked softly. "Have you heard that children and animals have great instincts when it comes to people?"

He shoved his hands deep into his pockets. His eyes were turbulent when he met her gaze. "Maybe they just don't know better."

Erin rose. "Oh, Garth." Not knowing what to say, she sighed, and followed her son's lead. Impulsively wrapping her arms around him, she wished she had the magic words to convince him.

He paused, then folded her closer.

Erin snuggled against him. "Well, maybe you're right. It *was* pretty rotten of you to teach him that *kyop* thing and tell him to practice it."

His chuckle rumbled against her cheek. "It's an important technique."

Erin pulled back to find a sneaky grin on his face. "So I'm supposed to be thankful?"

"Yeah." He nudged her backward until her back met the outer wall of the house. "Very thankful."

Her breath hitched in her throat, and she was caught between excitement and laughter. Wearing her most solemn expression, she said, "Thank you very much, Garth."

He shook his head. "Actions speak louder than words, lady."

"Oh!" A nervous laugh escaped. "You want me to show you how I feel about the fact that you've instructed my son to wake up screaming every day."

"I want a kiss, Erin." His gaze darkened with impatience, but the humor was still there. He pressed his pelvis against hers. "Now."

"I guess this means we've moved beyond the handshake stage," she managed to say. She felt powerful because of his arousal. Sweet and addictive, she wasn't ready to surrender it yet. She wanted to play. She wanted to tease a little. She cocked her head to one side. "Okay." She bussed him on the cheek.

His eyes lit with a warning fire. His gaze fell over her breasts and belly like a heat wave. "You're asking for it." He rolled his hips against hers.

Erin's breath caught. Her knees lost their strength. "It?" she asked in an unsteady voice.

He bent closer and tugged her earlobe between his teeth, then released it. "Don't worry. You're gonna get it. And I'll be the one to give it to you."

Erin closed her eyes and prayed.

Garth pressed his mouth to hers and kissed her until she was ready to tear her clothes off and beg for mercy. *Mercy* wasn't the word on her lips when he pulled away, though. Just a pleading whisper of his name.

Well, he'd screwed it up again Garth thought the following week at the Halloween carnival.

Since that night in her barn Erin had been kind and relaxed with him. He'd found a way to kiss her every night. Her response had him going home acutely aroused every night.

Painful but promising was the way he'd seen it. Until this afternoon, when he'd asked her a few questions about the hole in the fence, which led to a few questions about her past. She'd barely spoken a word on the drive to the center—"Thank you" and "We'll see you later."

Garth scowled at the Halloween carnival decorations.

"You're gonna scare that poor pumpkin to death, dear brother."

Garth looked up and cracked a smile at his baby sister, Carly Pendleton Bradford, who was dressed in huge waders and carried a fishing pole. "What are you doing here?"

Carly glanced around nervously. "Russ's idea. I told him I wished I could do more for the Children Who Have Lost a Parent group and he suggested I start with something simple. I'm taking a little break from helping with the Guess the Guts game."

Garth knew Carly hadn't completely resolved everything about the loss of their parents and that she was just as leary about discussing it as he was. He gave her a one-arm hug. "You okay?"

She took a moment to think it over. "Yes." Her face lit up in delight. "Yes, I am."

He felt a smidge of envy. "Good. Where's Russ?"

"Around here somewhere. He's dressed as a—"

"Don't tell me." Garth spied his brother-in-law across the hall. "A catfish."

"Yep," said Carly, hoisting her thumbs in her suspenders like a proud fisherman. "That's the one that *didn't* get away."

Garth rolled his eyes. "You're too cute."

"So is Erin Lindsey," she said in a teasing voice. Then she turned serious. "She's different. Don't mess it up."

"I already have."

Carly's face filled with consternation. "What'd you do?"

He felt a lick of irritation. "This isn't any of your business." When Carly set her mouth in disapproval, he shook his head, frustrated. "The lady's a little touchy about her past. I asked her a few questions and she's barely speaking to me now."

"You grilled her."

"I did not."

"Grilled who?" Their youngest brother stood behind them.

Garth turned to find Troy and Daniel closing in. Displeasure hummed through him. Just what he needed—a family intervention.

"Nobody," he said tersely.

"Erin Lindsey," Carly said at the same time.

"Oh." Troy nodded and gave a broad wink. "Garth's been spending all his spare time with her lately. Comes home smelling like perfume with pink lipstick on—"

"Did anybody ever tell you you've got a big mouth?"

Troy shook his head. "Touchy. Touchy."

Garth caught Carly fighting a smile.

"Speaking of 'touchy,' " Daniel said. "I think I just saw Ben Cantrell cornering Erin in the auditorium. You gonna do anything about it?"

That tore it. Between Troy the tormentor, Carly's interrogation, and big brother Daniel's unsubtle suggestion, Garth felt as if his privacy had been shredded, and he didn't like it one bit. Goaded, he struck out. "I'm not discussing this with you clowns. Especially you, Daniel. You sure as hell can't keep your eyes off Sara Kingston when she's around. When are you gonna take your own advice and do something about her?"

Daniel stiffened and shot Garth a killing glance. "I wasn't talking about Sara Kingston. I'm not the one who's coming home looking like a lovesick teen-ager."

Carly cleared her throat loudly. "Well." She smiled warily, still fighting her laughter. "If you'll excuse me, I need to get back to Guess the Guts. And I guess I'll leave you to, uh, your, uh, nondiscussion." She blew them all a quick kiss and scooted away.

It was ridiculous, Garth knew, but what he felt for Erin was private, still untried, and he didn't understand why, but he would rather slit his throat than share his feelings with anyone but her. He sighed, turning to Daniel. "So you saw her in the auditorium?"

Daniel cut his eyes at Garth. "Yeah. Cantrell was pitching hard."

"You've been a grouch lately."

Daniel frowned. "So have you." He crossed his arms over his chest. After a minute he shrugged. "Don't know why," he muttered in a low voice.

"I'll tell you why," Troy interjected, sticking his head between them. "You both need to get laid."

# SEVEN

In order to keep from ripping out Troy's vocal cords, Garth wheeled and headed for the auditorium. He heard the strains of a guitar and fiddle and noticed a sign: DANCING.

Garth was more curious about what was going on with Ben than he would confess. Although, he assured himself, he wasn't territorial about women, never had been, never would be. When he saw Erin backed up against the wall with Ben looming over her, however, that blithe notion about himself and territoriality where Erin was concerned fled forever. A cold, swift surge of sheer anger ran through him. The other laughing couples in the room faded into oblivion.

He watched Erin lift her shoulders and give Ben an approximation of a smile before shaking her head. Ben looked disappointed, but determined. He shifted his weight, and Erin took the opportunity to duck under his arm. But, Garth noted, the slimy SOB caught her arm. His blood boiled.

From across the room Erin's gaze chanced to catch his, her delicate features forming a pleading request for help. He automatically took a step forward, but the way she'd treated him earlier still stung. Garth narrowed his eyes and deliberately turned away. And who should appear at his side, all smiles and feminine invitation but Kendra Dillon? He'd bedded her last year.

"Hi, Garth," Kendra pouted prettily. "Long time, no see. You've been too busy to come visit?"

Garth knew this game. He'd played it forever. "I thought I heard something about you getting engaged a few months ago."

"I was," she admitted, catching his hand. "But I'm not now." Kendra tugged him closer. "I've missed you."

"Is that so?" Garth got a little rush from Kendra's attention. To hell with Erin Lindsey.

"Yeah." The band moved into a slow, make-out tune. "Wanna dance?"

She was asking for more than a dance, and Garth was in the mood to give it. But he felt an overwhelming wave of dissatisfaction that it wasn't Erin, then he shook it off and took Kendra into his arms. "Might as well."

It took ten straight minutes of saying no before Ben accepted the message. Erin finally escaped him and stumbled through the crowd only to plow right into a couple pressed intimately together.

"Oh," she said, backing away. "Excuse me. I wasn't watching where—" She broke off. Garth was the man in the couple she'd bumped into. And his partner was a voluptuous blonde.

She stood like a zombie trying to regain her composure. She couldn't hear the music for the roar in her ears, but she certainly could see—far too well in fact. Garth's right arm was draped over the woman's shoulder while his left hand pressed against her back, aligning her pelvis with his. The woman's generously displayed cleavage was offered up for his gaze.

Erin's insecurities about her sexuality raged to the surface. Angry, yet knowing she had no right to be, she flashed a glance at Garth's face. He looked surprised, but not at all miserable. *Why should he?*

"Erin," he began in that deep voice.

Lord help her, she didn't want to hear anything he had to say. Swallowing over the knot in her throat, Erin shook her head and forced a smile. "Sorry. Gotta find my son." Then she fled through the crowd.

Two hours later, having bummed a ride home for her and Luke with Carly Bradford, Erin lay in her bed staring at the ceiling. Luke was asleep. The only sounds were the rustle of her sheets when she shifted in her bed and the hum of the furnace when it came on. She looked away from the ceiling to her alarm clock; the green luminescent numbers flipped to eleven o'clock. All was well.

If everything was well, then why did her stomach feel like a tornado had touched down inside it? She felt a heavy, aching disappointment, the kind that didn't go away.

*Stupid.*

She closed her eyes. A few seconds passed and she thought she heard the hum of an engine. The hum got louder, turning into the distinctive roar of a familiar big black Harley. Her heart beat faster.

He had a boatload of nerve, she thought. Well, he could camp out on her doorstep all night and freeze to death for all she cared. She refused to answer the door. He was crazy if he thought she would speak to him at this hour.

The engine cut off.

She would have to be crazy even to consider talking to him.

A light knock sounded on the door.

Erin stiffened and held her breath. He would leave. The man had the attention span of a flea.

Another knock, this time louder, and Erin pulled the covers over her head. She would not answer that door. She would not.

"Erin."

"*Damn!*" Erin threw off the covers, jerked on her robe, and stalked down the hall. Keeping the chain connected, she cracked the door. "What do you want?" she asked, the sound of her voice harsh.

"I was supposed to take you and Luke home. I looked all over for you and couldn't find you. I was worried about you."

"Carly gave us a ride," Erin said, staring at the door. She didn't want to look at him. "Everything ended out okay. Good night." She tried to close it, but the toe of his boot stopped her.

"Let me in, babe."

His voice was different. If she didn't know him better, she'd say there was a wealth of emotion in that request. Who was she fooling? She didn't know him. "No."

"Why?"

She took a deep breath and looked at the ceiling. There were a million reasons. "I'm not dressed."

He swore. "I don't care. We need to talk."

She began to tremble, and it wasn't because she was cold. "Garth, it's late. You're letting in cold air and—"

"Honey, I'll keep the door open all night if I have to."

Her heart jolted foolishly when he said "honey." Resenting him for his effect on her, still she resisted the urge to stomp her foot and shriek at him. Instead she unlocked the door and quickly backed away. She wanted to put off looking at him as long as possible.

Garth stepped into the hall. Wariness surrounded Erin like a shield. Exhaling a heavy breath, he merely watched her for a moment. Her hair was tangled from being in bed. She wore a pink, soft-looking terry robe. He looked at her feet, and his heart twisted. She was wearing green argyle socks with holes in them. He might have chuckled if the emotional atmosphere weren't so charged.

"I couldn't find you after you left the auditorium," he began quietly.

She tied the sash of her robe a little tighter. "Luke and I spent a lot of time in the Haunted Room. He liked the screaming skeleton."

Her distance made him uneasy. "We agreed that I would take you—"

Her head snapped up, her brown eyes angry. "You were busy."

"I was jealous," he said, dropping the simple statement like a bomb.

Erin gaped at him. "Of what?"

He moved closer. "You and Ben Cantrell. I didn't like how he was all over you in there."

"I didn't like it either," she retorted. She paused for a moment, then her eyebrows furrowed in disbelief. "You didn't look jealous when you were dancing with that, that"—she shook her head, at a loss—"that woman."

Garth shifted, remembering his brief intention of taking Kendra up on her invitation. "Yeah, well,

I'm new at jealousy, but I sure enough was jealous as hell."

"Right." Her voice was full of disbelief. "You were pressed so close to that woman, you couldn't get a sheet of paper between your lower bodies. She's got a figure like—"

"Would you sit down and be quiet for a minute?" He took her shoulders, guided her to the sofa, and gently but firmly pushed her down. Catching her mutinous expression, he shoved his hand through his hair. "I'm not happy about this, Ms. Erin Lindsey. Not a damn bit happy. Just when I think we're getting somewhere, you get ticked off because you say I'm asking too many questions."

When she wouldn't look at him, he squatted down and put his hands on either side of her hips. "So, now you're not speaking to me. You want to tell me how you can find out what kind of man I really am if we don't talk?"

Erin opened her mouth, but he went on.

"Then I see Ben Cantrell practically groping you for the whole world to see." The memory of it still made him feel violent.

"*Practically* is the operative word," Erin managed. "You'd gone way past *practically* with what's-her-name."

He narrowed his eyes. "Which brings us to the subject of this ache for you that I swear I've had for half a century."

Erin snapped her mouth shut. Her cheeks flared with color.

"Nothing to say now. Huh?"

"Who was she?" she asked in a tense, quiet voice.

Garth's chest felt heavy. "Kendra Dillon. We were kind of involved last year."

Erin swallowed audibly and looked down. "She's beautiful."

"She's nothing." He shook his head. Unable to bear even this distance from her any longer, he picked her up and settled her on his lap. "Nothing compared with you."

The fight drained out of her. "That's hard for me to believe."

"Aw, hell, honey." He pressed her head to his chest. "I don't know what to say. I've never been jealous before. Never felt this way before. I swear I don't know how to act."

"Just be yourself and speak the truth. That would be nice." Her voice was muffled and shaky.

"Okay. Truth is I thought about going to bed with her." He felt her stiffen and rushed to explain. "I was fooling myself. I couldn't do it. I wanted you. Truth is I want you even if you don't want me. Truth is I'm so messed up over you, I don't know which end is up. And even though I'm the Pendleton Devil, I'm praying to God you still want me."

His heart grew heavy at the sight of tears in her eyes. "So tell me, Erin, am I the only one who feels this way?"

His expression was so grim, Erin thought. He looked as if he was bracing himself for the worst. It did something crazy to her to know that he was just as confused as she was. "No," she whispered. "You're not the only one. You know I want you."

He stared at her for a long moment, then put his hands to her face and slowly lowered his mouth to hers. The kiss was sweet, so sweet, she almost couldn't bear it, the passion humming, but banked. His mouth was tentative and searching, and she felt the tensed muscles of his arms beneath her fingers. Yet his warmth enveloped her, kindling the flame he seemed to start wherever he touched her. She was so moved by his tenderness, too, that she almost cried. She softly moaned, and gradually he ended the kiss.

Erin bowed her head and licked her lips, wanting to hang on to the taste of him. Dreamy from his kiss, she dropped her hands to his open jacket, clinging to it and rubbing her fingers over the soft leather. "What do we do now?" she whispered.

His chest swelled against the backs of her fingers as he took a deep breath. "I know what I want to do," he muttered.

She wanted to spread her hands across his bare chest, his bare body. She could feel his arousal pressing her bottom. Her pulse raced like an over-wound clock. "Yeah." She nodded. "Me too."

Garth went still. "You want to repeat that?"

Erin felt heat rise to her cheeks. "I want to make love with you." She looked into his face, and the sensual blaze in his eyes stopped her breath. She swallowed hard. "But not tonight."

Disappointment flickered in his eyes. "Still too soon?"

Erin bit her lip. "Not really."

"Afraid Luke will wake up?" He smoothed her hair.

She shook her head. "He's dead to the world."

His eyebrows furrowed in confusion. "Then what?"

She really didn't want to get into this again, but she supposed there was no way around it. "You smell . . . like *her*."

Garth closed his eyes. He swore, pulling her as close as he possibly could while their clothes were still on. "We're heading into deep waters, Erin. Don't pull back now."

"I didn't expect this. I didn't expect you." She shook her head, nuzzling his neck with her soft hair. "Sometimes I feel scared," she confessed.

"Yeah." Garth knew exactly what Erin was talking about. Sometimes he felt scared too. He put a thumb under her chin, lifting her sweet mouth to his, and he tried his best to kiss away the fear. For both of them.

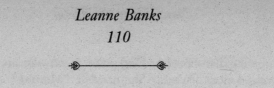

After lunch the next day Garth came and helped Erin work through a gait with Lily. She admired the rapport he was able to develop so quickly with the horse. The filly seemed to preen under his attention, doing her best to please him. When she displayed a bit of temper, he showed a firm hand in bringing her back in line.

One more reason to fall for the man, Erin thought desperately. She feared the stakes in a relationship with a man like Garth. Feared them, but felt compelled to risk a part of herself she'd never risked before.

Watching him murmur something low into Lily's ear and stroke her neck, Erin felt a dart of awareness. She immediately shook her head. The man was seductive even when he handled the horses? She needed help.

Garth caught her glance and gave Lily a whack on the bottom, dismissing the filly to cavort in the pasture. "That one's got a lot of personality." He grinned. "She's a peach."

"For you," Erin said. She watched him walk toward her with that sleek, easy strut, suddenly resenting his overwhelming masculinity. "Do you have that effect on all females? Crook your finger. Whisper a few choice words." She held out her arms in an exaggerated gesture. "Then just catch them when they fall like flies."

In an instant the grin fell away. A seductive, hungry look crossed his face. Capturing her with a gaze that said *You're mine, baby*, he crooked his finger. "Come here, Erin," he taunted in a voice that belonged in the dark between the sheets. "I'll catch you."

Her heart tripped. It was a dare. Everything about him was one big dare to her. His voice, his posture, his body, his personality all seemed to ask her if she had the guts to go the limit with him. He took a step toward her. Her stomach took a corresponding dip, and she reached the nervous conclusion that maybe she didn't.

She instinctively backed away. "Garth," she began, an uneasy giggle escaping, "it was just a crazy question." She took another step backward. "Forget I said a word." He kept coming for her and wearing that oh-so-serious expression.

A thrill ran through her. Muffling a shriek, she turned and bolted. The paddock gate was closed. For a second she considered jumping the fence. He was behind her, though. His warm breath on her neck sent anticipation down her spine. She scooted to the left. His predatory chuckle singed the ends of her tingling nerves. She scooted again, not watching where she was going, and ended up, out of breath and out of luck, one foot away from the fence.

Cornered.

He stood at her back, not touching her, yet the heat of his body was branding her back.

Erin swallowed. It was silly, but she didn't want to face him. In the oddest way, she was aroused. Maybe it was the chase, playing with him. Maybe it was just him. Either way she felt vulnerable and foolish. She walked to the fence and draped her hands over the post, breathing deeply.

Two breaths later his hands were on her shoulders.

"Why did you run?" He nuzzled her ear and rubbed her arms. "You're not scared of me, are you?"

Erin trembled. "A little."

"And?"

"And no," she said honestly.

He laughed, dropping his hands to lace his fingers between hers. "You don't have anything to worry about, Erin." His voice deepened. "You knew I'd catch you."

She felt the brush of his hardened masculinity against her bottom and sucked in a deep breath. "Is that supposed to reassure me?"

His tongue skimmed the edge of her ear. "It is," he purred.

Her joints were losing their stiffness. Her heart was flying faster than the favorite in the Kentucky Derby. "Garth," she began in a faint, husky voice.

He rubbed himself against her again. "I've got this problem, Erin. Every time I'm around you, I start thinking about what you look like with your clothes off. Then I start thinking about touching you. Pretty soon, in my mind, I've ditched my own clothes, and I'm inside you."

Erin closed her eyes. Her body was a mass of unslaked arousal from the tips of her breasts to the warm moistness between her thighs. She, too, saw the picture he drew. She saw it and wanted it. She bit her lip against a moan.

"I keep thinking about how you'd feel, all hot and wet." He sucked the lobe of her ear into his mouth, gently nipping it as if he were punishing her for tormenting him. Tightening his fingers around hers, he braced her against the fence, nestled himself between her legs, and moved in a searching rhythm that stroked and caressed.

The swelling, yearning sensation sent dizzying waves of teasing pleasure through her. Yet the teasing brought a fine edge of panic too. Her throat closed up. "Garth." She needed to touch him. She couldn't explain it, but she needed to touch him. It had to be now and it had to be intimate.

"I wish you were naked right now and I was pumping inside—"

Erin pulled her hand free and slid it behind her hips, reaching for him. His breath hissed out of his mouth with gratifying force.

He leaned against her, filling her hand with his denim-covered hardness. "Oh, God," he said when she cupped him and squeezed. "What time does Luke get home?"

Busy, and weak, and hot, Erin tried to concentrate on his question. She licked her lips, staring unseeing at the pasture before her. "Three-fifteen."

Garth glanced at his watch and went very still. A long silence passed as Erin continued to caress him. "Twenty-three minutes," he whispered harshly as if he were debating his possibilities.

What possibilities? she wondered frantically. They couldn't stop now.

He cursed and held her hand against him for a long moment, then pushed away from her.

Erin's knees buckled. She fell, feeling as if she'd been going sixty miles per hour and hit a solid wall.

Garth heard the soft thud of her body hitting the ground. Alarmed, he swiftly turned and gathered her in his arms.

Confusion marred her features. "What?" She swallowed. "Why?"

His loins throbbed. "I'm gonna need all night with you. Twenty minutes won't cut it. All night, Erin. Inside you."

Her eyes swept closed. He could tell she was trying to compose herself, but her body was burning up as badly as his was. Unable to resist, he brushed a soft kiss against her lips. She trembled. She was past arousal. He considered releasing her zipper and slipping his fingers into her core to give her some release, but his control was shot, and he wondered if she'd feel embarrassed afterward.

He made a quick decision and pulled her to her feet. "C'mon."

Erin struggled with boneless knees. "What?"

Garth tugged her along, out of the pasture.

"Where are we going?" Erin was doing her best to come back to reality.

He brought her to a stop in front of his bike and turned around with an ironic grin on his face. "We're going for a ride."

Within a moment Erin found herself on that big black bike her legs spread to accommodate Garth's hips. Her arms were wrapped around his torso beneath his leather jacket. She could feel the heat of him; she still hummed with wanting his touch. *Get a grip.* "I don't see how this is going to help," she muttered.

"Trust me," he said, knocking back the kickstand.

Erin felt a wave of trepidation. She'd never ridden a motorcycle. "Garth, I don't like—"

The engine roared to life. Erin jumped, instinctively clutching him tighter.

"That's right," Garth said over his shoulder. "Hold on tight and lean into the curves."

Before she could respond, they surged forward down her dirt driveway. It was all bumps and grinding vibration until they hit the road. Then Garth spiked the accelerator and swooped toward his family's land.

Struck dumb by the speed, Erin crammed her head into his well-muscled back and prayed.

"Loosen up," Garth yelled. "Enjoy it."

Erin glared at his back. *Enjoy this death machine?*

After a couple of minutes of hiding, though, she grew curious and peeked out. Half-plucked trees of November, wooden fences, and a cow here and there flew past her in a blur. She saw a sparkling, silvery stream and could almost taste its clear, cold water. The smell of fresh hay mingled with Garth's masculine scent. The bike vibrated beneath her. Amazing. All her senses were engaged.

He took an S-curve. She shut her eyes again as the bike tilted on the curve.

The sun shone down, but wind lashed at her cheeks and whistled through her thick denim jacket. Uncomfortably cold, Erin suddenly understood the therapeutic effects of the bike ride.

Garth slowed the bike to a stop and turned to face her. He pushed up the visor on his helmet. "What do you think?"

"I think I'm freezing."

"That's the idea. Better than a cold shower." He cocked his head. "Admit it, Erin. You've been wanting to ride this bike since the first time you saw it."

Her eyes opened wide. "I have not. I haven't touched it. Haven't even walked close to it."

"But you wanted to."

Her face was still cool, but she felt an insidious warmth spreading up her chest. She swallowed, realizing he was right. "They say people pick cars to suit their personalities. This one seems to fit you.

Dangerous, powerful." She gave him a wary glance. "Fast."

His gaze pinned her like a blue laser. "So why'd you come?"

She could say he'd coerced her, but it wouldn't be quite true. "All right," she conceded. "It fascinates me. All that speed and power."

"Yeah." Garth knew they weren't talking about the bike anymore. Maybe they never had been.

"I wanted to see what it would be like."

He felt an instant tightening in his loins and nodded. *You will, lady.* He sucked in a deep breath of air, hoping its coolness would reach his nether regions. "My cabin's a little farther down that way. Past the bend."

Her face brightened. "Can we go?"

"Not today. Not enough time." He paused, seeing her disappointment, then he followed an impulse. "Let's go out Saturday night."

Erin blinked. "Out? Where?"

"On a date." Garth grinned. "You know, dinner, dancing."

Erin opened her mouth to negate the dancing, then promptly closed it at the look on his face. The Pendleton Devil was uneasy. It was just a flicker in his eyes and the slightest shift on the seat. Her heart took a dip.

Saturday. This Saturday. Carly had commented on the drive home from the Halloween carnival about

Garth's upcoming birthday and how he never let anyone help him celebrate. In spite of Erin's anger at the time, the date had stuck. *This Saturday*.

She sighed. Surely for such a special evening she should be able to manage a few dance steps. "It sounds nice," she said. "I'll get a sitter for Luke."

Resentment sliced through Garth at her hesitancy. Instinct prodded him to shred her resistance like a veil. But no. That wasn't what he really wanted. He wanted Erin to shred that veil of trepidation herself. This was something new for him, the way he wanted her defenses to vanish. He usually preferred women to keep a few walls up. It made leaving easier. The Lord knew he didn't let any woman past his own defenses. How ironic that he wanted her defenses to vanish while his remained intact.

With Erin, though, he wanted nothing between them—not thoughts or inhibitions . . . or anything. And it would happen, he swore.

"Good. Real good," he finally said, but he was thinking of how it would be between them . . . soon.

# EIGHT

Perspiration beaded Erin's forehead as she concentrated on her feet. "A waltz," she told her uncooperative limbs. "Anyone can do the waltz."

At least that was what Miss Snyder had told her over and over again. She drew in a deep breath, absently smelling the hay-scented air in the barn.

"One-two-three. One-two-three." The radio music had a consistent, natural rhythm. Her feet did not.

From the crack in the doorway of the barn, Garth watched Erin struggle. Her fine eyebrows were set in deep furrows while her usually mobile lips were etched into a grim line.

Swiping a strand of hair away from her cheek, she continued her footwork. "C'mon," she muttered in frustration. "You've only got two days."

She stood stiffer than a poker with her arms rigidly outstretched to her imaginary partner, stomping in one-two-three time. He winced at her efforts, wondering how much time she'd spent in the barn trying to dance. He remembered a statement she'd made about dancing a few weeks ago.

Here she was trying to dance, though, to please him.

He stared for a full moment. By the tense set of her body, and her complete absorption, Garth could tell this effort was painfully important to her.

It was so sweet, it made his heart ache.

When had anyone ever worked so hard to please him? When had anyone cared enough to try? His throat tightened around an unexpected lump of emotion. He heard her swear under her breath, so earnest that he nearly threw open the door to run in and gather her in his arms.

It was a revealing moment, telling the tale of how Erin really felt about him, intimate enough that she'd probably rather Garth watch her undress than watch her attempt to dance. But he couldn't tear himself away, even out of respect for her privacy. He kept his gaze trained on her, absorbing the little drama to store forever in memory—the memory of a woman who cared for him.

A powerful sensation of pleasure and pain gripped him, taking his breath, because at that moment he realized that what he felt for her went way beyond caring.

Silently he backed away from the doorway. He

bowed his head, squeezing his temples. His heart raced. His brain protested. Oh, Lord, what had he gotten himself into?

How had it happened? Garth asked himself. How had that sliver of reticent feminine sunshine slipped into his heart? He'd spent the last seven years wondering if he even had a heart.

The one time he'd allowed a woman to get under his skin, he'd gotten burned and run off to Denver, which had only brought more trouble. Being responsible for Tom Calloway's death had deeply altered something inside Garth. Within an hour of when he had watched Tom fall lifelessly to the floor, he had begun to replay the scene with an eye to seeing how he could have handled it differently. Over and over, his mind punished him with the doubt that he could have made a different move and Tom wouldn't have died. Ironic, Garth thought yet again, that saving his own life meant taking another's.

Now, what he wanted more than anything was to forget that he'd killed a man . . . even in self-defense.

But it wasn't the kind of thing he could forget.

A bitter taste filled his mouth.

Garth considered breaking the date and staying the hell away from Erin. Anything between them was doomed. He wasn't the kind of man to stay with a woman. She was the kind of woman to cling. His gut twisted at the thought of her clinging to someone else.

A pungent curse broke the silence, then the muffled sound of Erin kicking wood—a wall? A stall door? Amusement flickered, but swiftly died. He had to decide damn fast what he was going to do about her.

At the least he had to help preserve her pride, he thought, whistling loudly as he went again to the barn door. "Hey, Erin," he yelled, loud enough to wake the dead. "You in there?"

Erin froze. *What was Garth doing here?* Had he heard her? Worse, had he seen her? Erin moaned. *Oh, God, please*, she prayed. *Don't let him have caught me.* She scrambled for the broom, fanning her cheeks at the same time. They were probably the color of tomatoes. "Yes," she called breathlessly. "I'm here."

He stepped in and took a quick glance at her pink cheeks, pasted-on smile, and white-knuckled grip on the broom handle. She was so charmingly disarrayed, his heart lurched. "Thought I'd come by and work with Luke after school today," he said. He glanced at his watch. "The bus comes in about ten minutes, doesn't it?"

"Yes. I was getting ready to go get him." Avoiding his gaze, she gave a few brisk, unnecessary strokes with the broom. "Just had to finish sweeping."

Garth nodded, moving closer. "I've been thinking about Saturday night," he began.

Erin's head shot up, relief and disappointment warring in her expression. "Oh." She cleared her throat. "I have too. You know, maybe it would be better if we didn't—"

Garth put his hands on her shoulders, pulled her against him, and kissed her. Too damn greedy to let her go, he dipped his tongue into the sweetness of her mouth, again and again, until his body grew taut and hers grew soft and yielding. He lifted his lips from hers, approving the dazed look in her eyes. "I just wanted to make sure that six-thirty's okay."

She took a shaky little breath that made him feel undone. "Okay."

He kissed her again, knowing he wasn't playing fair. He could see Saint Peter writing down another black mark on his record. But how could a devil play fair, Garth asked himself, when he had a chance to hold sunshine in his hands?

The restaurant was charming and intimate with crisp white tablecloths, soft candlelight, and rosebud centerpieces, a roaring fire at one end of the large room, and, Erin braced herself every time she looked at it, a dance floor at the other end.

He'd eaten steak. She'd had the salmon. They were waiting for dessert. Erin was waiting for when she'd have to get on the dance floor.

She lifted the glass of Chablis to her lips and took a large swallow, hoping the wine would still the butterflies in her stomach. She glanced at Garth, still stunned by his appearance. Amazing what an awesome body could do for a tailored, conservative suit.

"You're staring again," he murmured.

She took another quick sip before putting the crystal glass down. "Sorry."

He leaned forward, keeping his voice low and making her light-headed with his intent blue gaze, "You wanna tell me what's going on?"

"It's your suit." She looked at his impossibly wide shoulders and shook her head. "I've never seen you in a suit before."

His eyes glinted, and one side of his mouth hitched upward. "That bad, huh?"

The purr in his voice was like an invisible hand touching her erogenous zones. Erin was beyond pretense. "Horrible for me," she confessed. "I can't look at you without forgetting how to breathe."

His expression changed. Surprise, then a flicker of need. "You picked a helluva time to say that." He looked at her lips and took a drink.

This evening had been terrible on her nerves. Indignation nudged her. "Excuse me. Next time I'll say you're ugly. Would that be better?"

He chuckled. "Might be safer." He reached for her hand. "We're in a room full of people. If you're gonna talk about forgetting to breathe, save it"—he rubbed his thumb over her wrist—"for when we're alone."

"There you go again," she accused. "You touch me and I feel like I'm stuck at the top of a Ferris wheel."

Erin was confused and frustrated, and fed up. "I don't like this, Garth."

"I'll see what I can do to make you like it." He lifted her hand to his mouth, kissed it, and released it. "Later." He tugged at his collar and glanced around the room. "Let's talk about something else."

She took a deep breath and searched her mind for a topic. "When did you learn karate?"

"College. I took it for credit one semester and got hooked." He looked at her curiously. "What about you and horses? When did you get started?"

"I was attending a girl's school, and equestrian studies was part of the program." She smiled, remembering. "In the beginning I was terrible. Couldn't keep my seat. But the instructor didn't give up on me, and pretty soon I was spending every available minute at the stables. I liked riding, but I loved training and taking care of the horses. Seeing the improvements they made gave me a rush. Guess it still does."

Garth didn't like not touching her. Tonight she reminded him of the tender pink rosebud on the table; she'd be as delicate to the touch, her scent as alluring. He took her hand again and toyed with her fingers. "Is that where you met Luke's father?"

He felt her go rigid. "Yes. I was lonely. He was nice to me." She looked up at him. "He wasn't a bad guy, only immature, not ready to be responsible for another person."

A ripple of anger ran through him. "Then he shouldn't have helped *make* another person."

"I'm glad he did. I'm glad I have Luke."

Garth felt the twisting in his gut ease slightly. "Yeah. I'm glad you have Luke too." It bothered him, though, to think of her going through the experience of being pregnant all alone. "Where was your father?"

She frowned. "He was busy. He had a demanding job." She bit her lip. "After I told him I was pregnant, he—well—he—died."

Garth paused. Something in her tone didn't sound right. "You say that as if your pregnancy and his death are connected. You don't really believe that, do you?"

She looked away. The clink of silverware and the soft drone of other conversations swam around them. Erin seemed lost in her own private pain. Alone. He felt a strange, overwhelming desire to share it with her. "Erin," he began.

She took a deep breath. "He was very angry when he learned I was pregnant." She shook her head. "Very upset. He . . . he couldn't bear it."

Sickening comprehension dawned, and he said the ugly word aloud. "Suicide."

"No," she said immediately, then seemed to think about it. "But it may as well have been."

The waiter arrived with two generous servings of Black Forest cake, and Garth found himself wishing they were anywhere but here. She wore such a lost, regretful expression that his hands itched to touch her.

When the waiter left, he said "Erin, you can't blame yourself for—"

She help up a hand and shook her head. "Please. I don't know how we got started on my father, but the day he died was the worst day of my life." She gave a tentative smile. "This is one of the happiest times. Besides, it's your birthday and—" Her eyes rounded. "Oops." She looked guilty as hell.

"Who told you?"

"Can I plead the Fifth?"

"Carly," he guessed, accurately if Erin's expression was any indication.

Erin reached for her purse. "Well, now I don't have to wait to give you your present." She pulled out a small package wrapped in festive paper, tied with a fat green bow.

Garth took it into his hands, ridiculously pleased.

"It's nothing much," she warned him, her face coloring. "I had a hard time choosing, and if you don't like it, feel free—"

"I'm not giving it back. You oughta know better than that. Once you give to the devil, he never gives back."

Erin felt a jolt at his possessive tone. He wasn't talking about her little present. She wasn't sure how to deal with his warning. "Open it."

She watched him tug the ribbon loose, then flick

his finger beneath the paper to give it a quick rip. It made her think of how he would undress a woman. Expertly, with breathtaking speed.

He looked at the jazz CD, then at her. "How'd you decide on this?"

Erin shifted slightly in her seat. If he knew her true rationale for selecting his present, he would think she was silly. The moody music had reminded her of his personality, and he seemed to have such an awareness of his body, she'd guessed that he might like it. "I thought you might like . . . like it."

"And?"

The man had the instincts of a hunter. He could sniff a hidden story a mile away, and he obviously wanted her to spill hers. *No.* She'd revealed enough tonight to make her feel vulnerable and fragile. "And I went with my instincts."

"You've got good instincts." He grinned suddenly. "I'm in the mood to dance. What about you?"

Dread fell over her like a wet blanket. "I-uh—"

Before she could finish, Garth flicked his hand to get the waiter's attention. "You can wrap up the cake. I'll take the check now."

Confused, Erin smiled weakly. Hadn't he said something about dancing? Silence grew between them. At last she dared to eye the instrumental combo at the other end of the room.

"Not here," he said, answering her unspoken question. He placed the money in the leather checkbook and nodded as the waiter returned with the wrapped cake. Garth turned his gaze on her. "We're going to my cabin."

Erin's heart bumped against her rib cage.

He stood and extended his hand. "Ready?"

She hesitated. *Ready for what?* With Garth it would be everything. She swallowed over the lump of anxiety and excitement in her throat. Again, following her instincts instead of good judgment, she slipped her hand into his and felt his strength and warmth.

"You're quiet," he said as he ushered her through the door of the cabin.

"It's dark." Erin tried to get her bearings.

He flicked on a table lamp and slid the CD into the player. In seamless movements he helped her out of her coat and discarded his jacket. A smoky saxophone eased out of the speakers.

Erin drank in the sight of the room, searching for secrets to his personality. They were easy to spot.

No television in sight, but the elaborate stereo system and large selection of CDs revealed his kinship with music. A wall of shelves housed a collection of books and equestrian journals. The decor was simple, almost stark, yet she thought that spoke of him also. He wouldn't want a lot of clutter in his life. A comfortable sofa stocked with pillows, a lounger, a woven rug, and he was content.

She saw only one hint of a need for softness—the flannel blanket folded neatly on the back of the sofa.

This was Garth's haven, she knew. And he'd brought her here. Her stomach took another deep plunge at the meaning.

He hooked an arm around her neck from behind. "You haven't wished me 'Happy Birthday.'"

Erin turned, smiling. "Happy Birthday."

He grazed her jaw with his thumb. His expression was utterly serious. "It is happy this year, thanks to you."

"You're welcome very much," she managed to say in a husky whisper. His mouth hovered close, oh so close to hers for a moment. She could feel his breath.

Garth closed his eyes in a bid for control. Or maybe it was a prayer of thanks. He was so moved by her and her tenderness. "Do me a favor."

"What?"

"Trust me, Erin. Tonight, just trust me."

Her wide brown eyes were full of the same thing he was feeling. She swallowed and nodded.

His heart speeded up. The sound of the sax wove around him. It was an aphrodisiac, though he didn't need one with Erin.

She'd given him music to make love by. He wondered if she realized it. The rush he felt was so strong, it reminded him of popping a wheelie at a dangerous speed. His chuckle came out a little unevenly.

"I'm gonna take off your shoes." Garth dropped to his knees and eased the black heels from her stockinged feet.

Erin couldn't speak.

He ran his thumb down the sole of her foot, feeling a lick of humor threaten when she curled her toes. Her stockings were sheer, silky. He followed the urge to let his hand climb her shapely calf, around the back of her knee and up her thigh to where lace met warm, tender skin. Her soft gasp fluttered against his hair.

She leaned forward and gripped his shoulders. "Garth?"

Her hair fell in a blond curtain around her face. Her thigh trembled against his hand.

The urge to tear off that silky stocking was strong, but the lazy music reminded him there were other things to take care of first. All his needs would be met tonight, he knew it, felt it with the strength of a man who'd gone without tenderness most of his life. "Later. There'll be more later," he murmured to her and to himself.

Kissing her thigh through the dress, Garth inched his hand away. He rose and steadied her, taking care so that she wouldn't lose her balance. "You okay?"

"Dizzy. I feel a little dizzy."

The corners of his mouth lifted. "Yeah. Well, that'll get worse."

Erin wasn't quite sure how she was still standing. When he'd touched her thigh, she'd nearly melted.

Her heart already had. She watched him drop her shoes into the lounger, then ease out of his own and kick them aside. After ditching his tie, he reached for her hand and pulled her into the center of the oval rug.

"Time to dance."

Erin stiffened immediately. "Okay." Praying she wouldn't ruin things, she lifted one unsteady hand to his shoulder and with her other prepared to take his hand.

Garth drew both her hands and pulled her flush against him. "Around my neck," he instructed her. His other hand fastened around her waist.

"I'll step on your feet," she protested, her heart sprinting.

"That's the idea." He lifted and pulled her to him so that she had no choice but to stand on his feet.

With her brain clicking along at such slow speed, it took a moment, but the light dawned and Erin flinched at the sting of humiliation. "*You knew.*" Her voice caught. "*You saw,*" she said accusingly.

Disregarding her distress, he nuzzled her ear. "Saw what?"

Her face was hot with shame. He was going to make her say it. Pushing against him, she said, "You know. You saw me trying to dance in the barn."

Garth's chuckle rumbled down her nerve endings. "Is that what you were doing?"

Erin gasped, staring at him. His face was all gentle humor and affection.

"I thought you said you were sweeping." He blew her bangs, distracting her. "Now, stop talking and stand on my feet. It's my birthday, and you're supposed to grant my every wish."

*Every?* Erin shook her head. "Garth, I can't—"

He put his finger over her mouth. "Hush. You haven't had the right teacher."

"This is crazy," she muttered, his nearness playing havoc with her emotions. "I feel silly."

He slid his big hands up, pressing her as close to him as was possible. "Just pretend your body and mine are one."

Slowly Erin extended her arms and twined her hands around his neck. The hair at his nape taunted her. There was a space of silence, then another sexy song meandered out of the speakers.

"Ready?"

"I guess."

"Close your eyes."

Erin obeyed, and Garth began to sway. Wrapped in his strength and heat, she followed where he led. From one side to the other, he gently pulled her while the music swelled. No words, yet she was steeped in him. It was as if he transfered his movement into her body. Her face buried in his neck, she inhaled his scent with each breath. His heart thumped against her chest. His belly rubbed hers while her abdomen cuddled his masculinity. A gentle nudging and shifting and it wasn't long before she felt swollen between her thighs.

"Lift your head."

Drowsy with him, everything about him, she did as he said. When her gaze met his, her heart stopped. His eyes were so full of need and tenderness, it hurt to see.

"You're beautiful, Erin Lindsey," he whispered.

She didn't have time to shake her head in denial. His head descended, eclipsing the light. His lips meshed with hers while his hand played lightly up her rib cage to her breast.

Sighing, she touched her tongue to his. She ruffled her fingers through his hair and caught his groan in her mouth.

His mouth grew a little less careful, a little more greedy.

Erin thrived on that small loss of restraint. Placing her hands on either side of his head, she kissed him with all that was inside her, tasting him, sucking his lips until they were both breathless. She swiveled her hips against his arousal.

"Oh, lady." Taking a quick breath, Garth caught her hips with his hands and moved her against him. "What you do to me." He tipped her chin back and kissed her neck with moist, warm lips.

Erin barely noticed that the music had stopped. Her senses were too preoccupied with Garth. She heard the whir of a zipper and felt cool air on her back. Her dress fell off one shoulder, and in a move too smooth and quick for her to call, Garth's hands lifted her skirts and cupped her bottom while he lifted her high.

"Wrap your legs around me."

Although his fingers clasped her buttocks with gratifying need, Erin wasn't too sure about it. But then his mouth was sliding beneath her neckline to her breast. "Oh," she exclaimed softly. Her skirt rustled as she clung to him for dear life. Pushing past her flimsy bra, he found her hard, aching nipple and sucked it deep into his mouth.

Erin's breath left her. She clutched at his muscled arms. Her instinct to be naked and intimately connected to him overrode everything else. She pulled at his buttons. "Garth."

He heard the tearing desire in her voice, felt it in his heart and gut. "It's okay, babe," he reassured her. "There's more to this dance. We haven't even begun."

He swung her around in his arms and carried her to his bedroom. He left the door open so that the soft light would shine into his dark room, the way she was shining her special light into his dark heart.

Gently easing her down his hot, ready body, he snatched kisses like a man who'd never kissed before. He tugged the dress over her head and saw the threat of modesty cross her eyes after he stared at the sight of her breasts in the lacy bra.

She gave a shy smile, looking down at her plumped-up breasts. "Amazing what an underwire bra can do, isn't it?"

He shook his head, wondering how he could feel like laughing when he wanted inside her so badly, he ached with it. And he knew she'd worn that scrap of push-up lace for him. Cupping her breasts with his hands, he deftly released the front catch. "It's beautiful, but I like what's underneath better."

The panties followed. He stilled her trembling body with a kiss that nearly blew his gasket and melted her into a puddle. He toyed with those black lacy garters as she finished off the buttons to his shirt.

Erin buried her face in his chest and inhaled. She groaned.

"What is it?"

She kissed his warm skin, ran her lips over a flat nipple, feeling his swift intake of air. She let her hands trace his ribs down to his belly. "Nothing is close enough."

His whole body shuddered. "You're hell on my self-control."

Erin bit her lip and looked at him, feeling desperation and desire back up in her. "I don't want your self-control," she said in a shaky voice. She unbuckled his belt and pressed her open mouth to his chest.

The first garter popped free. In seconds the stockings were sliding down her legs like water. Amidst a few heated, desperate kisses, Garth shucked his slacks.

He pressed her onto her back, and finally they were skin to skin. They both moaned into each other's mouths, restlessly arching and shifting. Her hands didn't know where to go first: his bare back, his chest, his narrow hips.

His hands, however, seemed to know all the right places to go: her breasts and belly, between her thighs where she was damp and far too empty.

He teased the secret nubbin, which sent an electric shower through her nerve endings. She arched against him, wanting so much, she hurt. Instinctively she reached for the hardness that unequivocally demonstrated his need. He was big and warm in her caressing hand.

Garth let out a hiss of breath. "Stop," he choked out. "Give me a minute."

Somewhere along the way Erin had shed her shyness. She kissed his neck, lingering over his salty taste, and continued to rub him. "A minute's too long."

He swore and reached for the bedside table. "Ten seconds." He ripped the foil packet.

All the while, her hands were busy tangling in his hair, her lips busy with his mouth, more hindrance than help.

Garth took control then, pushing her back against the pillows. She was hot silk and wet satin and she wanted *him*. Her brown eyes were dazed with the fever of need for *him*. Her thighs shifted restlessly against his, whispering entreaty for release from *him*. His heart and body swelled with exquisite pride and need and passion.

He spread her legs wide, carefully watching her eyes. Trust, desire, and something more welled within the bottomless depths of her brown gaze. Something that froze his lungs and warmed his soul. The urge to mate with her was overwhelming.

He probed against her slick opening and watched her eyelids drop to sultry slits. Her breath came in uneven puffs, her body undulated in irresistible womanly appeal.

The provocative movement undid him. Garth thrust forward into her tight femininity and took the deepest plunge he'd ever taken. Deep into her sweet, warm waters. Her moan mingled with his.

Erin strained against him, her head rolling from side to side on the pillow. "I've been waiting for you for weeks."

"And I've been waiting for you forever," he muttered, moving with long, smooth strokes, in and out of her. The catch of her breath made him sweat. The way she hung on his arms as if she'd be lost without him brought the first drop of honey to the tip of his arousal. A wild groan rumbled up from his depths.

"Oh, Garth," she said helplessly, arching into him. Higher and higher he went, everything inside him tightening like a twisted, bare, electric wire. The first jolt knocked him breathless. With the second, oblivion set in. Erin. There was only Erin with the sweet mouth and gentle hands. Only Erin with her welcoming body.

She milked him, on and on, with her tiny inner clenches until Garth was struggling for reality and air, and he knew he'd seen heaven for the first time in his life.

# NINE

Erin slowly opened her eyes, expecting the walls of the cabin to be in a pile around her. Amazingly the beams supporting the ceiling were still there. And they weren't even shifting from side to side.

Garth breathed heavily against her shoulder. She trembled.

He kissed her neck, sucked the tender skin, and she closed her eyes again. He was still inside her. Her legs were still wrapped around his waist, and she couldn't have moved a muscle if she'd had to.

Garth did it for her, reluctantly rolling to the side and pulling her tight against him as if he couldn't bear any distance between them. The thought caused her stomach to tighten with all the emotion that had risen within her during the last hour.

Bare and intimate, she lay snuggled into his chest, his legs twining with hers. He nuzzled down to her ear. "Stay the night."

His hands began a smooth stroking motion up and down her side. His thumbs grazed the outer edge of her breast, sending a tingling to her nipples. She bit her lip at the sensations rushing through her, plunging her into a state of readiness again.

Hooking his thigh around hers, he swiveled his hips against hers. He lowered his mouth to give her a long, lazy kiss while his thumbs traveled the rest of the way to pluck at her beaded nipples. "Garth," she gasped.

"Stay the night. You've been making me hungry for a long time." His warm lips found a nipple and tugged, sipping and licking at the crest. "I'm not anywhere near full yet."

Erin felt a sharp contraction of yawning desire. Her inner thighs grew damp. But when he edged his mouth down to her belly and lower, her mouth went dry. "Garth," she said, fighting unbearable excitement. She pushed at his shoulders. "Stop. You've got to stop."

He paused and looked at her. "Why?"

*Yes, why?* her body asked impatiently. She shook her head. "The baby-sitter." She worked to steady her wispy voice. "I've got to be back by midnight."

His gaze slid to the alarm clock by the bed, and he ran a hand over his eyes. "It's eleven-thirty, and it'll take twenty minutes to get there." For a long moment he looked at her as if he were considering saying to hell with the sitter and ravishing her anyway. Instead he took a deep breath and shifted his shoulders to release the rippling tension. "We'd better get dressed."

He eased off of the bed and offered a hand to assist her. Erin accepted, wondering who this act of denial was costing the most. Her knees dipped under her own weight.

Garth caught her. "Not quite steady yet?"

The gentleness in his tone turned her emotions helter-skelter again. Erin was caught between laughter and tears. She swallowed hard. "Not quite."

She felt too many things at once—incredible desire for him again, sweet weakness at his tenderness. She wanted him so badly, it was embarrassing. So she was stuck, hot with need, flushed with self-consciousness. She ducked her head at his intent gaze.

"Hey, what's going on in there?" He pulled her against his hard body.

"Nothing."

"Don't lie, Erin. You're no good at it."

She closed her eyes. "I'm embarrassed."

"Why? I've seen all of you, and you can be damned sure I liked every inch—"

"It's not that. I just—" She shook her head, wishing she didn't feel so messed up. "I just—oh, damn."

He gave her a gentle shake. "Just what?"

"I still want you." Erin swallowed hard, looking at him helplessly. "See how my hands are shaking? And my breasts?" She lifted her hands. "And I'm all . . ."

Garth's gaze heated with the same arousal. "And you're all hot and wet." He kissed her firmly. "For me."

"Yes," she admitted. "Worse than before."

A rush of satisfaction poured through him, hovering around his heart and settling in his loins. "That's because now you know how good it is between us. Give me your hand, Erin." With wide eyes she hesitantly complied, and he wrapped her hand around his full arousal. His breath hissed out when she ran her thumb over the head. "See what you do to me? Don't ever be embarrassed about wanting me, baby."

She was like a flower unfurling, her sexuality a mystery she was only beginning to explore and accept. He wanted to be the man to know all the facets of her personality. He wanted to be the man she turned to— for everything. It was a strange hunger, leaving him both aroused and faintly displeased.

Feeling himself thicken with each passing second, he eased her hand away. "You've got an ache, and I'm just the man to take care of you." He hesitated and backed away from her. Seeing her uncertain expression, frustration ran through him, and he shoved a hand through his hair. "I'd kiss you, but with you standing there in nothing but your skin, I'm long on want and short on control. Do me a favor and get dressed."

A smile grew slowly on her face, starting with the lips, then shining through her eyes. "Speaking of skin ..." Her gaze flicked over him in frank, undiluted admiration that had his body temperature soaring again. "I don't want to blink."

"Erin," he said in a warning voice.

"Honest." She shrugged, and her small breasts bobbed. "I'm afraid I'll miss something."

He groaned, turning his back to her. "Hell."

They managed to get dressed and out the door in three minutes. Garth refused to help Erin, saying he needed to keep his hands off of her. Erin huffed a little, but they made it home with five minutes to spare.

Garth gave the teenage baby-sitter a ride to her home and quickly returned. He pushed open the door, and hearing sounds from the kitchen, he headed in that direction. He stopped short at the sight that greeted him.

Erin and Luke stood over a cake placed in the middle of the table. They both turned to him with matching, expectant brown gazes.

"Happy Birthday, Garth!" Luke said.

Erin wore a long-suffering expression. "He woke up the second you left to take the baby-sitter home."

With the energy of a child gleefully playing past midnight, Luke jabbed another candle into the cake, then hopped down from the chair. "Isn't it neat? Mommy made it and let me decorate it."

Garth felt his throat tighten. It might be a small thing to another man, a homemade birthday cake, but it hit him harder than a bad fall from a wild horse. Luke took his hand and pulled him to the table, giving a running commentary on the cake.

"I picked out the Ninja man and the motorcycle," Luke said, pointing to two of the three figurines on the top. "Mommy picked out the stallion." Luke licked some white frosting off one of his fingers. "We both did the words, but I did all the trees. Flowers would have been sissy."

Garth looked at the squiggly odd-sized letters forming the word *Happy*, the straighter letters for *Birthday* and *Garth*. The "trees" were triangular blobs of green and yellow. It was easy to see who'd done what. His chest contracted so painfully, he wondered if he was having a heart attack.

"Not exactly Black Forest cake," Erin murmured.

"What do you think?" Luke tugged at Garth's pant leg. "Isn't it the neatest, very best cake you've ever seen?"

Lord, what could he say? The last time he'd had a birthday cake made especially for him had been years ago. Occasionally Carly tried, but Garth usually made himself scarce on his birthday. No one, he thought in amazement, other than his sister Carly or his long-deceased mother, had ever done anything like this for him. Erin seemed to find each one of his secret empty places to fill.

He swung Luke up in his arms. "Yes. It is without doubt the neatest cake I've ever had or seen." He hugged the precious little boy to him and looked at Erin. "Better than Black Forest. Thank you."

"You're very welcome," Erin said with a grateful smile.

Luke hugged Garth back, then wiggled to get out of his arms. "Can we eat it now?"

"Just a minute," Erin said, lighting the candles. "Garth has to make a wish and blow out the candles." She shook out the match flame. "Ready?"

A wish. The first thing that sprang to his mind left him speechless.

"Happy birthday to you," Erin and Luke sang together.

Their voices swam around him in surrealistic notes, bouncing off his disoriented mind. He wanted this for more than a night, more than a day.

*It'll never happen*, the devil inside him said.

He wanted the headaches Erin and Luke would bring him.

*You're crazy.*

His dark soul craved the laughter.

*Laughter always turns to tears.* The devil's voice grew fainter.

Erin eased his pain.

*She'll turn on you.* A last, desperate bid for protection.

The hard core of his bitterness splintered, and in that instant a seed of hope grew. Erin wouldn't turn *on* him, not if he always gave her a reason to turn *to* him.

He needed her love.

The silent admission sent him reeling.

The singing stopped. "Make a wish, Garth," Erin prompted.

He looked into her warm brown gaze, and the turbulence inside him stopped. He made a wish.

Thirty minutes later, after they'd each eaten a piece of cake, Erin managed to get Luke into bed. She'd expected him to be wound up and difficult, but he talked nonstop for three minutes, then drifted off to sleep in the middle of a sentence.

Smothering a chuckle, she eased his door closed and made her way down the hall. A hand shot out from her bedroom, surprising the breath out of her. "What—"

Garth gathered her to him and shoved her door closed with his foot. "Little boy all tucked in?"

She nodded, automatically yielding to his embrace. "Yes."

He sifted his fingers through her hair and tilted her face closer to his. "Then it's time for me to tuck in the mom."

His mouth encompassed hers in warmth, his tongue edged between the seam of her lips, and he was making her dizzy all over again. His arms tightened, and the flavor of the kiss became a little desperate. His tongue was seeking and finding, his mouth caressing and needy.

She felt bereft when he broke away.

"I—need—to know," he said in a husky voice.

She felt the hammer of his heart against her hand. There was something barely leashed about him that snapped and crackled in the air. It made her hot and weak and completely susceptible to him.

"Am I staying the night?"

Erin didn't hesitate. "Yes."

That little word had the same effect as shaking nitroglycerin. She saw it in his eyes first, the flame that cut loose and seared a path straight to her belly.

He kissed her as if he wanted to devour every inch of her. His hands were fast and urgent, slipping the top of her dress down and baring her breasts. A second later he was pulling up the hem of her dress. Without a pause his fingers slipped beneath her panties, searching for her moistness.

Erin gasped at the hell-bent speed, yet the thrill had her blood soaring through her veins. She tugged at his shirt buttons, and the sensation of his hard chest against her aching nipples made her cry out.

He slipped his fingers inside her.

Her cry became a low, keening wail.

"God, I want all of you, every way at once."

Her involuntary tightening around his finger drew a rough growl from him. Everything cut loose then. Her dress seemed to disappear. Distantly she heard the rip of her panties.

She was recklessly hurtling straight down a track to a place she'd never been, but there was nothing she could do—nothing she wanted to do—to stop it.

She was primed for his total possession. Whatever he wanted, she wanted to give. The relentless ache pounded in the tips of her breasts, low in her abdomen, and down where his hand wove a path of pure pleasure inside her. Erin tugged impatiently at the buttons of his jeans.

He pulled his probing hand away from her, and she whimpered in frustration. "Oh, baby," he muttered, holding her close. "Don't worry. I swear I'm gonna take care of you. I swear it. Just a little longer." He kissed his way down to her breasts and praised them with his tongue and teeth.

He skimmed his mouth down to her belly and knelt between her trembling knees.

His mouth touched her inner thigh, his intent clear. His hands rubbed her thighs as if to soothe, but the gentle strokes only made the ache worse.

He looked up at her, his blue eyes swallowed by black pupils exposing the depth of his need. "I want every inch of you, Erin. Every inch has got to be mine. I *need* to taste you."

She bit her lip, caught between the wildness of his desire and an innate fear of the unknown.

His breath puffed against the tender skin. "If you feel like you're gonna fall, grab onto me."

His head lowered, and her heart jumped into her throat. She whimpered when his lips glanced off her thigh. Then his velvet mouth found the folds of her femininity and Erin couldn't bear to look.

She tightly closed her eyes. Firmly grasping her hips, he searched for her hidden, swollen bead until she was a mass of exposed nerve endings.

She was an instrument he played, the crescendo building inside with each stroke of his tongue. There was so much he was expressing with every movement that it filled her to the point of spilling over.

If she didn't know better, she'd think he was gripping her as if she were the most important thing in the world. If she didn't know better, she'd think each sweep of his tongue said she was precious. If she didn't know better, the desperation emanating from him said he needed her more than life itself.

If she didn't know better, she'd think he loved her.

The notion sent her over the edge. She cried out his name. Like a wave swelling, she broke on the shore. Her knees dipped and she clasped his shoulders. A giant spasm shook her, then ripples of release took her on and on until she was weeping.

"I can't"—she shook her head helplessly, crumpling to the floor—"I can't—"

"Shhh," he muttered in a raspy, spent voice, catching her. He shoved his jeans and briefs down over his jutting masculinity. He licked his lips, seeming to relish her lingering taste, and pulled a packet from his pocket.

Her inhibitions burned to cinders, Erin took it from his hand and tore it open, then stretched the condom over his hard length, all the while locked in his heavy-lidded gaze. His chest heaved with the exertion of a long-distance runner.

Leaning against her bed, he opened his arms. She willed her body into his lap. He pulled her up and in one slick motion set her on his thickened masculinity.

Erin sighed.

Garth squinted, hissing an expletive between his teeth. "So damn good and tight." He hooked his hand behind her neck and drew her forward for a wet, blazing, tongue-tangling kiss.

"The only thing I regret is this damn rubber." His voice was low and uneven. "I want to feel the inside of you."

A shocking spurt of heat shot through her. Her wanting for him knew no boundaries. She struggled for a deep breath and had to settle for a shallow one. "I got"—he shifted beneath her, sending a shower of sensations through her. She swallowed hard—"a diaphragm last week."

A revealing admission, one she hadn't intended to make, but it seemed to please him beyond words. His eyes grew stormy with passion and he pushed deeper inside her. "Next time," he promised with a deep kiss that mirrored his body's movements. "Next time there won't be anything between us."

Then he began to rock beneath her.

The night passed in a haze of needy lovemaking. Every time they came together, Erin lost a little of herself to him. Garth made it his mission to learn every inch of her. It was a tender, yet ruthless act of possession, the way he barely let her touch earth before pushing her upward again. "No secrets," he whispered when she turned her head away at a particularly intimate question he'd asked. Then he'd taken her up and over again.

Sated, he held her in the dark. "I never wanted you to know this," he murmured in a low voice as he slid his hand over her hair, "but you're bound to hear the rumors sometime." He took a deep breath. "I"—he swallowed—"I killed a man when I was living in Denver. It was self-defense, but . . ."

His fading voice said it all, the anguish and pain he still lived with. Erin fought tears. She wanted so badly to rid him of that pain. At that moment she felt like a helpless fraud.

"I guess I wanted you to think I was somebody great. I—"

"Hush!" she managed to say in a husky voice. Her throat tight, she shook her head. "You *are* somebody great," she whispered. "And don't you ever forget it."

She held him tight and kissed his cheek, but deep down she had the unsettling feeling that he didn't believe her.

Erin didn't have time to ponder it all until just before dawn, when Garth slept beside her. *No secrets*. A chill ran through her. The vague sense of foreboding swelled into something more substantial.

She would always have secrets. She wasn't quite sure who she was protecting anymore, though. Luke? Herself? Garth? Pressing a hand to her forehead, she squeezed her eyes shut.

How could she tell Garth who she really was? Would he hate her for it? How would he look at her once he knew? She envisioned accusation in his eyes.

A lump rose painfully in her throat. A dry sob threatened. She couldn't tell him. It was cowardly, but she just couldn't do it.

Forcing herself to take a deep breath, Erin looked at him. He was strong even in his sleep, breathtakingly beautiful in his naked splendor. Vivid memories of how he'd possessed her shook her. The power of his passion made her feel bare and vulnerable, dependent on him for protection.

How could she hide from him now? she wondered desperately. Would he be able to read her deceit now that he knew her intimately? And if so, who would protect her?

An hour later Garth felt the first shaft of sunlight across his face. Even before he fully awakened, he knew Erin wasn't with him anymore. It was an eerie knowledge that pulsed in his blood and went deeper than his bones, making him restless during that last twenty minutes of semisleep.

He heard Luke's voice, then a gentle shushing from Erin. For a moment Garth wondered what it would be like if he were a permanent resident in their home. He wondered how it would feel if Luke called him Daddy. He wondered how it would feel if Erin called him Love. It was his closely guarded secret that he'd always wanted to be a good woman's "Love." He'd always wanted to hear someone special call him Love.

Fighting a sense of overwhelming foolishness, he nonetheless allowed himself to focus on the fantasy for a moment. The vision of Luke bounding into their bedroom waking him and Erin on Saturday mornings made Garth grin. Erin could bring him a cup of coffee. Or he could surprise her and bring her a cup.

The bedroom door opened, and in walked his fantasy wearing her terry robe and carrying a cup of coffee. Her cheeks were clean and pink, he supposed from the shower, but he noticed her eyes didn't meet his.

"Good morning. Hope you like it black," she said, setting the cup and saucer in his waiting hands. "Sorry I don't have time to fix you breakfast, but Luke and I are going to be late for Sunday school if I don't hustle."

"Thanks," he said in a deep voice that reminded her of everything they'd done in the night.

Nervous. Nervous. Nervous. The sight of him sprawling on her lavender sheets made her feel as if her soul was on fire. Her fingers were responsible for his mussed hair. His mouth was as swollen as hers. Her palms had explored every inch of his gorgeous chest revealed above the covers. Were those red marks on his shoulders from her fingers?

How mortifying.

Even more disconcerting were the pink beard burns she'd discovered on her body while showering.

Taking a deep breath, Erin opened the closet, pulled out a dress, then rummaged through a drawer for underwear and stockings. She really had plenty of time, but being in Garth's presence made her feel a little crazy. The silence was unnerving, so she filled it. "Luke hates to be late, especially since the teacher brings doughnuts. He's afraid he'll get stuck with one of the jelly-filled ones. I don't remember Sunday school teachers serving doughnuts when I was growing up." Her hands full of assorted clothing, she turned. "I wonder if more adults would come to Sunday school if they served—"

Garth stood directly in front of her, completely nude.

Her mouth went dry. For the first time in her life Erin appreciated the term "good as sin on a Sunday morning."

He leaned over with a sleepy grin and kissed her. "Let me help you."

Erin resisted the urge to run her tongue over her lips to savor his taste. "Help me what?"

"Get dressed." He lifted a garter belt from the pile. "This first?"

# TEN

Erin gaped at him. She shook her head to clear it. "I said get *dressed*, not *undressed*."

"I know," he said calmly, moving the clothes from her arms to the bed.

"Garth, I'm in a hurry and I really can dress myself just fine." She pressed her lips together.

"I know." He leaned closer and kissed her cheek. "But I really do want to help."

Her reserve melted a little. "Why?"

He shrugged, and the rippling of his muscles made her catch her breath. "I guess because it's personal." He loosened the belt of her robe. "And I want to be personal with you this morning."

Erin felt her blood heat. "We can't—"

He pressed a finger over her lips. "I know. Don't worry." He looked down at the pink undergarment in his hand, then back at her with a raised eyebrow. "This first?"

She sighed, feeling alternately confused and cared for. "Yes," she finally said, still full of reluctance.

In deference to her modesty he left the loosened robe on and kneeled down for her to step into the pink swatch. Then he eased the garter belt up her legs and over her bottom, his fingers lingering only a second or two on her waist.

"Bra?" His voice was a little rougher.

Her own breathing was uneven. She nodded, wrapped in the intimacy of his gaze.

He pushed the robe from her shoulders and stared at her breasts for a long moment. Erin closed her eyes. She couldn't look at him. Her breasts were throbbing, and he hadn't even touched her. She felt the straps of the bra beneath his warm hands sliding up her arm to her shoulders.

A pause full of anticipation and restraint had her holding her breath.

"Just one touch," he whispered, and she felt his mouth on one nipple, then the other.

A shot of pleasure shimmied through her. She trembled. "Garth," she whispered.

"It's okay." He cleared his throat, fastening the front clasp of her bra. "What's next?"

Erin's eyes flew open. "Stockings. I'll do the rest. Really. I—"

"Let me."

Erin groaned. "You're going to make it very difficult for me to keep my mind focused on the minister's sermon."

He grinned. "Well, it's obvious what I'm thinking about."

Erin bit her lip, letting her gaze lower to the evidence of his desire. "Why are you doing this when you know we aren't going to-to finish?" She balanced herself by holding onto his shoulders. "Why are you torturing yourself?"

He gave her a gentle shove onto the bed and stilled her with a gaze of unadulterated possession. "If touching you is torture, baby, then go ahead and pull out the rack, 'cause nothing's gonna stop me from it."

She had no response for that. Her heart hammering in her chest, she realized she didn't want him to stop.

Expertly rolling up one stocking, he stretched it over her foot.

His ease with the task provoked her, and she frowned. "You're awfully good at this." She straightened her foot to help him. "Have you done it before?"

He looked at her in surprise. "Dressed a woman? Hell, no." He bent her knee and smoothed the stocking the rest of the way up her leg. Fastening the garter, he started on the other one.

Erin gazed at him skeptically. "For someone who has never done it, you're very adept."

His mouth lifted in a killer grin. "Thank you."

Erin rolled her eyes, fighting the pleasure his undiluted attention gave her. The sight of his large, masculine hands wrapped around her delicate lingerie made her feel as if her privacy had been invaded—and she loved it.

He fastened the other garters, slipped on her panties, and skimmed his lips over her thigh, chuckling at her gasp. "Sorry," he said without an ounce of repentance. "Couldn't resist."

Somehow he made the crazy situation seem as if it were the most normal thing in the world. Erin lifted her arms for the slip. She hadn't received this kind of care since she was a child. Garth's tenderness felt more intimate than ever.

He pulled her to her feet and slid the dress over her head. "Turn around so I can zip it." After lifting her hair from the collar, he zipped it. "Where's your brush?"

Erin shook her head. "I can brush my own—"

"I know, but I—"

Erin sighed. "But you want to." She waved her hand. "It's on the dresser."

She would have dragged the brush quickly through her hair with little concern for pulling at her scalp. Instead Garth used the brush carefully. With controlled, gentle strokes he smoothed the tangles until her hair hung in a shining curtain around her face.

He looked at her, warmth and affection glowing in his eyes. "Done. All you need are your shoes."

She was having trouble with this. She didn't know what it meant. Afraid and charmed at the same time, she tried for a smile. "Feels kinda strange to be all dressed up with you—"

"Naked as a jaybird," he supplied with relish.

She let out a breathy laugh. "That wasn't the exact comparison I was thinking of."

He put his hands on his narrow hips and raised an eyebrow. "What was it?"

Lord, he was cocky. Deservedly so, she thought, wanting to touch him, put her arms around him. Giving her itchy hands something to do, she grabbed a fabric hairband from the dresser and slid it onto her head. "I was thinking that if the government knew how good you look nude, you'd need FDA approval," she said, keeping her tone dry.

He took her hand and swung it between them, his blue eyes growing suddenly serious. "The better to please you."

The lighthearted mood was stripped away. Something darker and deeper hung between them. On shaky ground, Erin felt uncertain and hesitant, yet compelled. She lifted her hand to his rough cheek. "I don't know what to say," she whispered. "I've never felt like this before."

Closing his eyes, he turned his mouth into her hand and kissed her palm. "I want in, Erin, in to every part of your life. Don't cut me out."

Her stomach twisted. She bit her lip at the

wrenching sensation inside her. It was the one thing she couldn't give him. She wished things were different. She wished she were someone else.

"M-o-m!"

Luke's voice brought her back to reality with a resounding crash. She glanced at the clock. "I've gotta go." Looking at Garth, she felt the ridiculous urge to cry. An achy, vulnerable sensation settled in her chest. She looked away, blinking furiously.

He must have read her distress. "Hey, come here." He pulled her into his arms. "What is it?"

For just a moment she absorbed his strength and deeply inhaled his scent. For just a moment she luxuriated in embracing him. The moment passed, and she made herself pull away, feeling a sense of loss with every inch she put between them. "I'm not sure I can explain it."

Catching the concerned expression in Garth's eyes, Erin avoided his gaze and quickly moved toward the door. How true, she thought, her guilty conscience lashing at her. There was so much she couldn't explain.


Over the next week Erin found herself torn between living for the moment and accepting all Garth offered, and pulling back to protect both of them. Making love hadn't eased her desire for him. It had heightened her emotions and awareness of him. And she suspected that he was as tuned in to her emotional shifts as she was to his.

She wasn't the only one frustrated by her shilly-shallying. Garth had even gone so far as to ask her bluntly what time of the month it was for her. Erin wished she could use premenstrual tension as an excuse for her behavior.

Luke fed and in bed, he grilled her over dinner. Same questions. She gave the same nonanswers. Which started the same argument. Then he left in a huff, roaring out of her driveway while she fought back tears.

She took two aspirins and decided to call it a night. Deceit was damn tiring. Her mind full of warnings, she wrestled with her problem as she had every other night this week.

What should she do?

*She should cut it off and back away.*

How, she asked herself angrily, how could she cut out her heart and keep living?

Silence. The same dark and damning silence settled over her like the night, leaving her with the same helpless feeling. She closed her eyes against it, breathing deeply, forcing the thoughts from her mind until she fell asleep.

*Bang!*

The loud sound jerked her straight up in bed. She clutched the sheets to her chest.

*Bang!*

An explosion of breaking glass followed the sound. "*Bitch!*" a male voice called out.

"Mo-o-o-mmy."

The distressed sound of Luke's voice galvanized Erin into action. "Stay in bed, Luke. I'm coming."

She scrambled out of bed and stumbled toward his room. Bullets. It must have been bullets. Trembling, she heard another shot and more glass shattering. Too scared to breathe, she pushed Luke down on his bed and held him tight.

Her whole body tense, she waited for more, but the only sound she heard was the gunning of an engine and the squeal of tires. The metallic taste of fear filled her mouth. Luke began to cry.

Erin squeezed him, rubbing her unsteady hands over his tense little body. *Oh, God, what should she do?*

Fifteen minutes later the sheriff and deputy arrived at her doorstep. While the deputy frowned at the shattered picture window, Erin gave Sheriff John Blackwell a replay of what had happened and the other, previous incidents. The sheriff, however, must have sensed that her nervousness went beyond the most recent act.

"Is there someone you want Ed to call? A neighbor or somebody?"

Erin took a deep breath. She was still trying to stop shaking. "Garth. Garth Pendleton."

The sheriff gave a nod to the deputy, and Ed went into the kitchen.

Blackwell pushed his hat farther back on his head. "Ms. Lindsey, you haven't lived around here very long. Where'd you live before you came to Beulah County?"

Erin bit her lip and adjusted the blanket she'd wrapped around Luke. Uncharacteristically quiet, he sat on her lap, his little arms plastered around her waist. "We moved here from out west."

Blackwell pulled up a chair and sat down in it. "Where out west?"

Erin hesitated, wishing with all her heart there was some way to avoid this.

"Ms. Lindsey," the sheriff prompted, "I need to know the facts if I'm going to catch the people doing this to you."

"I know." She smoothed Luke's cowlick and turned her head to one side. "Will this information be kept confidential?"

Something flickered in his eyes. "From the media?"

"From everyone."

He shrugged. "The only people who'll know will be connected with the department."

Realizing she had no choice, Erin took a deep, fortifying breath. "We lived in Denver."

He nodded slowly.

"My last name used to be Calloway."

He narrowed his eyes. "Any relation to Tom Calloway?"

"Yes. He was my father."

The first overt slice of emotion passed over his face. His gaze widened slowly in disbelief, then he shook his head. "Does Garth know?"

Her heart in her throat, Erin couldn't form even that small word. She couldn't even shake her head. But the shared knowledge of what Garth had done and her subsequent deceit hung between them.

He let out a long hiss and pulled off his hat to slide his hands through his hair. "Lady, you've got yourself in one hell of a mess."

She knew. Oh, how she knew.

Blackwell quickly quizzed her about her life in Denver and let her know he'd be calling her with more questions. By unspoken mutual agreement he switched the direction of the conversation when Garth arrived.

Garth looked like an avenging angel, his eyes a mix of concern and fury. His gaze locked with hers, and he went straight to her side. "Are you and Luke okay?"

Garth wrapped his arm around her shoulders, and Erin felt a sudden easing inside her as if she would be safe now. "Yes." She managed a half smile. "Shaky, but okay."

"She shmushed me," Luke piped up, peeking out from the blanket. "When they used guns, she shmushed me."

"She did?" Garth chucked Luke's chin. He could envision the scene with disturbing ease. Heedless of her own safety, Erin would always put Luke first. She would put her body in front of any bullet fired in her son's direction.

A cold chill ran down his spine at the thought of losing either of them. He felt Erin's troubled gaze on him and gave her shoulder a squeeze at the same time he ruthlessly yanked his emotions under control. Later. He would deal with that later.

Lightening the mood, he gently pinched Luke through the soft blanket. "It feels like you've still got all your stuffings."

Luke giggled, then his eyebrows drew together in a frown. "Mommy, why did that man yell 'bitch'?"

Garth watched Erin's face pale. He felt a heavy thud of anger pound through his veins.

"Someone yelled that right before he fired the last shot," she said. "I'd forgotten."

Garth took her hand and linked his fingers through hers.

Blackwell frowned. "Did he say anything else? Did you hear anything else?"

Erin shook her head, concentrating. "No. But the engine of the car he drove didn't run smooth. It was loud."

"Maybe a bad muffler."

"I don't know." Erin turned to Luke. "Honey, I think the man yelled 'bitch' because he was mean and angry. It's a word that nice people don't say to a lady."

The stress of the evening was beginning to show on Erin's face. Garth pulled Luke onto his lap. "You two can stay at my cabin." He left it open-ended because he wasn't sure when he'd feel comfortable about them coming back to this house.

"Thanks," she murmured, rubbing her forehead.

"One last question, Ms. Lindsey, did you see anything, anything at all?"

Erin shook her head wearily. "Nothing. I stayed in Luke's room for five minutes after the last shot was fired."

"We counted to sixty," Luke offered. "Six times. Mom said I counted too fast."

Blackwell's lips twitched. "You've got a little trooper there."

"I know." Erin gave a weak smile.

The sheriff faced Garth. "You might not want to ask her too many questions tonight. She looks done for the day."

Garth nodded. "I'm putting them both to bed." Determination swelled inside him. Damned if he was going to let this happen again. "I'll be calling you tomorrow."

Blackwell's eyes slid away. "Just let us take care of this one, Garth."

"I—" He stopped at the touch of Erin's hand on his arm. Her eyes pleaded with him, making him struggle to rein in the instinct to go after the bastard immediately. Later, he promised himself, taking a deep breath. "Let's get you two out of here."

Sheriff Blackwell gave Erin and Luke a ride to the cabin while Garth drove his motorcycle. Garth made a fire, and after a cup of hot chocolate and some exploring, Luke settled into bed. Garth watched Erin stand in front of the blazing fireplace, staring into it. Her arms crossed over her chest, she appeared restless yet weary at the same time.

Garth put his hand on her shoulder and guided her to the sofa. "C'mon. You're worn out."

She collapsed beside him, burying her head in his chest. Her arm crept around his waist. He went weak with tenderness when she curled herself so close, she seemed to want to absorb him. "Wanna talk about it?"

He felt a negative shake of her head against his shirt. The fire gave a loud pop.

"Wanna talk about anything?"

Another negative shake of her head, and Garth was pretty sure he knew what Erin needed. He stroked the hair away from her forehead, then gently moved his fingers to her eyelids and temples. She gave a soft sigh and began to relax.

"Thanksgiving's coming pretty soon, then Christmas," he said, keeping his voice low and easy. "When my mother was alive, we used to call it 'turkey' month because of all the leftovers. We might have the whole family together this year. The twins, Ethan and Nathan, finished work on their doctorates last spring. Did I tell you about them?"

"No," Erin murmured, melting into him a little farther.

"If we can nail down Brick, that'll be everyone. Wonder who we'll rope into fixing the turkey?" He kept on talking about unimportant things, judging her feelings by the pliancy of her backbone. Right now she was just this side of melted butter. "It'll probably be a cold winter, but then spring will be here before you know it and your lady mares will be dropping their prize babies left and right."

He paused, checking her breathing. Even, restful. She was asleep. He shifted her into his arms, and even though he wanted to hold her all night long, he carried her into the bedroom where Luke slept. She'd promised Luke she'd be in later.

She stirred when he removed her shoes. He eased the blankets over her and hesitated, hovering over her for a moment. She'd turned into every good dream he'd ever had; she fulfilled every secret desire. Garth brushed a kiss over her cheek and held his breath at the rush of emotion that flooded him.

Erin turned her lips to his, sweetly offering. His mouth gently touched hers and he pulled away. Still not completely awake, she whispered, "I don't deserve you." Then she turned her head and feel asleep.

For a long time Garth stood over them, frowning

at what she'd said. The uncalculated statement made his gut churn. Why would she think she didn't deserve him? It was the other way around. He didn't deserve her. He didn't deserve anything as good as she was.

Uneasiness pooled in his stomach, making him want to hold her close again. A ruthless determination rose up in him. He had Erin and he wouldn't let her go.

He'd find who shot out her windows. He'd find him and make sure he didn't do it again.

Erin poured the sweet feed into Rapunzel's bucket. The mare had already finished a healthy serving of fresh hay. The munching sounds the horses made gave Erin a measure of peace after last night. The man following her every move, however, contributed to her nervousness.

Garth shook his head. "I think it's a bad idea for you to stay at your house tonight. What if that bastard comes back?"

Erin stiffened, fear slicing through her. She deliberately shook it off. "The sheriff doubts he'll be back tonight. I can get the window fixed today. I told you before," she said, turning to face Garth, "I don't want Luke disrupted by this any more than necessary."

Garth's eyebrows drew together in a heavy frown. "Luke didn't mind sleeping at my cabin last night. You didn't mind sleeping there, did you?"

"No," Erin assured him. "And I can't tell you how much I appreciate everything you've done for us." She stepped closer, trying to make him understand. "But your cabin isn't our home. This is." She felt her resolve strengthen. "I'm not going to run. Not anymore."

Garth cocked his head to one side, narrowing his eyes. "What do you mean—not anymore?"

He didn't miss a thing, she thought, trepidation casting a shadow on her hard-won courage. She bit her lip, wondering when she was going to commit the ultimate slip-up that would cause everything between her and Garth to fall apart. She turned away and brushed off her hands. "I mean, this is my home now, and I don't want to be chased out of it." She paused, her heart sinking at the thought of losing Garth, though she knew it was inevitable. "For any reason."

"I don't like this."

She started to open the barn door. "I'm sorry."

He slammed it shut and turned her around to face him. "Dammit, Erin. Listen to me." He gripped her shoulders firmly, his blue gaze sending off sparks of anger and something more difficult to define, something that grabbed her and wouldn't let go. "You could have gotten hurt last night. Do you know what the thought of that does to me?" He shook his head. "This is serious."

She took a deep breath. The power emanating

from him put her off kilter. She closed her eyes. "I know it's serious." The words squeezed their way out. "I know I could have been hurt last night. Luke too." She opened her eyes. "But I wasn't. He wasn't. And life goes on." A sad memory assailed her, but she smiled anyway and touched his cheek. "I've got to do this my way, Love."

Garth stared at her, too choked up to respond. *She'd called him Love.* It took him a full minute to remember to breathe. He would have asked her, begged her, to say it again, but he couldn't find the words.

*She'd called him Love.* He swallowed hard. When he finally spoke, his voice sounded rusty to his own ears. "I don't want you hurt. I want you safe."

"I will be."

It wasn't enough. An idea nudged at him, and he decided to act on it. "If I can't be with you every minute, then I want to be sure you at least know what to do in an emergency."

Erin looked taken aback. "I know how to dial nine-one-one."

"That's not what I mean. If a man comes at you—" He paused, fighting a dark rage. "If a man comes at you, I want you to be ready."

Her gaze slid away. She shrugged uncomfortably. "I don't think that's likely to happen. And if it does, I know there's not that much a five-foot-six-inch, one-hundred-twenty-pound woman can—"

"Yes, there is. You can poke out his eyes, crush his windpipe, or yank his—"

She gave him a squeamish look. "Garth!"

Feeling a scrap of impatience, he frowned at her. "You can't fight fair. You've got to hurt him." He stopped, remembering for a moment. "Unless he has a gun."

Something came and went in her eyes so quickly, he couldn't identify it. "There's *nothing* you can do if he has a gun."

"Nothing *you* should try." He gave a rough sigh. "This is important to me. So even if you don't like it, I want you to pay attention."

"But—"

"Please."

Still uncertain, she nodded. "Okay."

He tightened his hands on her shoulders. "Pretend I'm coming after you. Pretend I'm trying to hurt you."

Erin felt a shiver of trepidation at the lethal look in his eyes. It was as if he'd changed identity in a second from lover and protector to a man who could kill her with one flick of his wrist. "Garth . . ."

He stepped closer, his gaze narrowing. "Do it."

Swallowing hard, she swung her fist at his face. He caught her wrist like a vise in a motion so fast, it was a blur. She paused, staring into his ruthless face.

"You can do better than that," he goaded.

Her heart began to pound. She swung the other fist, harder, faster, but he still caught it.

"Whatcha gonna do now?" he asked in a not-so-nice voice. "Scream? Cry?"

He played the part of ruthless attacker all too well. Erin didn't like being caught and held against her will. She liked it even less when she realized her real attacker wouldn't be Garth. A bubble of anger rose to the surface. Her breath caught and she kicked his shins hard.

He flinched, but in another one of those invisible moves, her hands were trapped behind her, and her body was pressed too close to his for kicking.

She wiggled and struggled for all she was worth, damp perspiration beading between her breasts. "Damn!"

"One out of three's not bad for the first time," he muttered. "I'm gonna let you go. Then we're going to try this again." He looked meaningfully at her. "My way." He let go and backed away. "First, don't try to fight like a man. You'll lose."

His arrogance nettled her. "That's chauvinistic."

"That's reality," he retorted, and held up her fist. "What kind of damage do you think this fist is really gonna do to a man's face?" Her hand looked small and fragile inside his larger, calloused one. "You hit a guy in the face, chest, or gut with this and it won't even faze him."

"I believe," Erin said between gritted teeth, "I just told you I knew I couldn't do anything."

"And that's where you're wrong. You just can't

choose the traditional method." He shifted forward and took her shoulders again.

Erin stiffened.

A quick glint of approval flashed in his eyes. "Good. You're taking me seriously."

"I've always taken you seriously." She meant it in all ways, physically, emotionally, and every other way known to man and woman.

A dry grin tilted his lips. "I'll ask you more about that later. For now slide your fingers through my hair on either side of my temples. Look like you're going along with me. You hate my guts," he crooned, "but you're giving in."

Erin did as he said, twining her fingers through his silky black hair just as she'd done so many times before. The action brought a haze of pleasurable sensory memories. "Now put your thumbs over my eyes," he coached.

Hesitantly she positioned her thumbs over his eyelids, studying his black, stubby eyelashes. She'd never done that at leisure before. They'd always been too busy doing other things.

"Think about the position of your hands. Feel it. Memorize it. If this were for real, you would have jabbed your thumbs into my eyeballs and pressed hard into the sockets. It's like pushing your fingers clean through the shell of a cantaloupe."

Her stomach lurched, and she removed her hands. "Lovely."

Garth ignored her. "Your third choice is to cross your thumbs over each other like this." He lifted his hands showing her the correct position and tossed her a no-nonsense look. "Do it."

Erin glared at him, but did it. "Is this a new way to fight off vampires?"

His lips twitched. "Not exactly. Press your thumbs against the base of my throat."

"Is this necessary?"

"Yes. I want you to feel where you need to push, so you'll know what to do if you need to."

Tentatively she pressed her crossed thumbs to his throat.

"Down a little bit," he said in a quiet voice, standing very still.

Erin adjusted the position of her hands.

"That's where you need to push. A guy can't hurt you if he can't breathe." He watched her pull back her hands, wearing a disturbed expression. He wanted to hold her and tell her she'd never need to know these things, but something deep inside him wanted her protected even if he couldn't always be the one to protect her. "Just two more things, Erin."

He watched her gather her resolve. She brushed her hand through her hair, then crossed her arms over her chest. "Okay. What's next?"

"You grab him by the"—he searched for a term that wouldn't offend her—"the family jewels."

Her eyes widened, then she looked at the ceiling.

Garth frowned. "Did you hear—"

"Yes, I heard you. I'm supposed to grab him by the *family jewels*. You want to educate me on technique?"

He hesitated at her terse tone, then went on. "Get a firm grip and yank downward."

"Am I supposed to practice on you?"

"Hell, no."

"Why not?" Her color high, Erin shot him a challenging look and took one step closer. "You've made me practice everything else."

# ELEVEN

Unable to tell whether Erin was kidding or not, Garth shifted at the subtle change in her. Just a glimmer of her feminine power emanated from her. It was alternately exciting and alarming. A lick of heat traveled up his throat, and he resisted the urge to pull at his collar. "I think you're familiar with the location of that part of a man's anatomy."

She shrugged, but he saw the shimmer in her eyes and finally understood. He'd pushed her just a little too far.

"I knew where your eyes were and where your throat was," she pointed out, "but you still wanted me to experience it."

When she took another step closer, Garth was caught between the urge to drag her to him and the opposite urge to back away. Somewhere along the way the control had slipped from his hands.

"Don't I need to *feel* where I'm supposed to pull downward?" she asked, turning his instructions back on him.

"Shouldn't I," she lowered her gaze to his loins, then arching her brow, she looked into his eyes, "*experience* it?"

The thought of her hands on him packed a punch of arousal. Her audacious, out-of-character dare grabbed hold of his gut, and all his primitive instincts rose to the surface. He knew she wouldn't hurt him. The self-defense lesson could wait. He was getting hotter and more curious with each passing second. Just how far would she go?

"Okay, babe, you want to experience it?" His voice sounded gravelly. "I'm waiting."

Without a trace of uncertainty Erin met him dare for dare, stepping close enough to feel his body heat pulse against her. The last week had just been too much for her. Between her spiraling relationship with Garth and her terror from the recent vandalism, Erin had been pushed too far. Her emotions had been driven from one end of the spectrum to the other, and she wanted, no, needed to call the shots about something.

Garth's lesson in self-defense pointed out her helplessness, even though he was trying to give her tools to protect herself. Her feelings of vulnerability, frustration, and need bubbled within her like the contents of a witch's caldron. Her skin felt pulled too tight, as if she were ready to overflow. For once in her life she needed to say when and how—and it needed to be now.

She placed her palm on his thigh, stretched taut beneath the worn denim. Running her thumbnail up the inseam, she watched his eyes narrow to slits. His fists hung by his sides. She stopped just short of her goal.

His shudder gave her a rush of power, and she cupped him with her palm.

He sucked in a quick breath.

"Is this right?" she asked.

"Yeah, but if I were an attacker, you'd grab tighter."

Erin gave a gentle squeeze. "Like this?"

His eyes widened. "Yeah. And you'd pull down hard."

Erin paused for a moment, thinking about how vulnerable Garth was right now. He'd done it deliberately—made himself vulnerable to her as if he understood what was going on inside her. She studied his face, trying to read him, but all she sensed was a coiled waiting. "But that's not what I want to do right now, is it?"

He gave a dry chuckle. "I sure as hell hope not."

Releasing him, she spread her fingers in a **V** and slowly moved them up his hard length. "What if I want to do something else?"

He pressed himself against her hand. "It's your experience, babe. You call the shots."

Her stomach churned with excitement. She felt

her breasts grow heavy and she lightly stroked him again. Stretching up on her toes, she whispered close to his lips, "I didn't know the Pendleton Devil could take orders."

"As long as Erin Lindsey's giving them." His mouth obliterated the tiny space between them.

Erin kissed him then, and the give-and-take of their tongues burned away any stray doubts and hesitation. He let her set the pace, male following female. She felt spurts of pleasure all along her nerves. She didn't want to need to breathe; she only wanted to kiss him forever, plastered against his chest.

A little moan escaped her, and she pulled at his shirt. She kissed the spot where his pulse leapt beneath the skin of his neck. Of its own accord her tongue sneaked out to caress him while her fingers released his shirt buttons.

She buried her face into his chest, breathing in his scent, wanting to absorb it. "I've always liked the way you smell."

His heartbeat pounded against her cheek. "How's that?"

"Like a man," she murmured, finding his flat brown nipples with her tongue.

"Erin!" he whispered harshly. "Let me touch you." His hands still hung by his side.

"Not yet." Erin knew once he touched her, she'd surrender and melt into a puddle. She wanted to relish playing the role of sensual conqueror a little longer.

Her busy fingers undid his belt and jeans. The zipper's hiss mingled with Garth's groan. He was huge and hard in her hands. Arousal settled like a burning brand low in her abdomen. Erin felt the swell of all her secret places, the liquid yearning, the edginess of frustration.

Her hands began to shake, and she let out a sound that was part sob, part laughter. "You might have to educate me on technique again." Bending, she slid her mouth down to replace her hands.

"Sweet Lord, Erin." Garth shuddered under her lips. "Let me touch you." Her tongue flicked over his taut, tender flesh, and he clenched his jaw, fighting the urge to let go and thrust.

"Am I doing okay?" she asked, her breath flowing in soft little pants against him.

"You do any better or any longer and I'm a goner." He lifted his hands to just above her head. "Let me touch you, babe."

The pleading note must have gotten through. She raised her head, her eyes dazed with such passion and love that his knees nearly buckled. "Okay." She swallowed. "I only want to please you, Garth. I only need you to know what you mean to me. . . ." A look of intense anguish crossed her face. "No matter what happens."

His heart was so full, it crowded his chest. He could scarcely breathe. With a single-minded desire to wipe away the fear he saw in her eyes, he lifted her up so that he could kiss her precious face. "Nothing's gonna happen to you. I won't let it." He began to peel away her clothes. "I swear it. I want to protect you."

His hands drifted over her like a warm wind. "I want to love you. I want to marry you."

He smothered her gasp with his lips. Her heart seemed to stop in her chest. She almost thought she'd heard wrong. Her emotions jerked from ecstasy to guilt. But with heart-rendering passion Garth brought her focus completely back to him. He made her his, and Erin committed every heated whisper, every loving touch, every melting, telling gaze to memory and died a little inside.

Later that day Erin called her lawyer in Denver. He sympathized with her situation, promised to offer any assistance when the sheriff called, and reminded Erin she would receive a dividend check from one of her father's investments in the mail.

Troubled, she hung up the phone, watching the workmen repair the picture window. With Garth at the Pendleton farm and Luke at school, she took a few minutes for herself to ponder who was behind the vandalism. She wondered if it could be one of her father's former business associates. Lord knows, she'd received enough threatening calls after his death.

Erin realized long ago that not all of her father's business dealings had been on the up-and-up. That knowledge had added one more sorrow during her pregnancy.

When the threatening calls and the whispers about her father's violent death persisted, she'd changed her name and moved out of her father's house and into a home for unwed mothers. She simply couldn't tolerate the idea of Luke having to bear the burden of her father's crime.

After drifting through the first years of Luke's life, living on her inheritance and learning how to be a mother, Erin had arrived at a time when she couldn't drift anymore.

When her lawyer had informed her that her father's lease for a horse farm in Tennessee was up for renewal, some of Luke's little friends started asking about Luke's daddy. It had hit her hard, and she'd known deep in her heart that it was time for a fresh start.

She still hadn't figured out how she'd ended up so close to Garth Pendleton. The coincidence—or the accident of Fate—was mind-boggling. Her strong feelings for him, though, made the questions recede now. Frowning, she concentrated again on who was responsible for the bullets.

"If you're that miserable about being here, maybe you ought to stay at my cabin."

Garth's voice immediately brought her out of her daze. "I'm not miserable." She led him into the kitchen. "I'm thinking."

"You looked miserable." He handed her a small

stack of letters and leaned against the doorjamb. "Brought in your mail."

"Thank you." A thick silence settled between them. Erin felt his gaze, heavy and thoughtful. She sensed they were both remembering what he'd said earlier and that nothing had been settled between them.

If she were anyone else in the world, they might stand a chance to share something long-lasting, but though Erin could change her name, she couldn't alter the fact that she was the daughter of the man Garth had killed. She'd resolved it in her own mind and didn't blame Garth. If Garth ever found out, he wouldn't be able to look at her. She knew it. She bit her lip at the pain that shot through her.

She loved him, but she couldn't have him forever. She also wouldn't be able to send him away. He would have to be the one to leave. She would never have the strength to send him away. A lump of dread formed in her throat.

Needing something else to focus on while she tried to compose herself, she sifted through the pile and pulled out the dividend check from her lawyer. "There it is," she muttered to herself and put the mail on the counter. She finally glanced up at Garth. "Coffee?"

He nodded. "And straight talk."

Her stomach jolted. She nodded, and poured coffee into cups.

"I want you to tell me everything that happened last night."

Erin sighed. "You already know. Some guy fired off a few shots, yelled, then hauled out of here. The sheriff told me the bullets were from a hunting rifle."

Garth rubbed his lip with his thumb. "Could have been a kid, then. Has Blackwell talked to those two teenagers who work for you? They might know something."

Erin handed Garth a cup. "I'm sure he'll be thorough."

When Garth remained silent, contemplating the situation, she added for emphasis, "I'm confident Sheriff Blackwell will take care of this expediently."

Slipping his gaze over her like a rope, he turned his head to one side. "Everyone can use a little help now and then."

"Garth," Erin began, "you know what he said."

"Could this have anything to do with someone in your past?"

Erin stiffened. A trickle of desperation threatened to turn into a gush if she didn't find a way to shut it off. She turned away. "I have no reason to think that. Either way, John Blackwell will check out all the possibilities. You don't need to worry about it."

"Babe, I'll be worrying until the guy's behind bars. If you have even the slightest suspicion that your past could be involved, you'd better cough up the information now."

Erin dumped her own coffee down the drain. She

couldn't have forced anything down her throat at the moment.

Garth was suddenly behind her. Gently he turned her around, his gaze earnest as he looked into her eyes. "I meant it when I said I wanted to protect you. I wasn't playing around."

She struggled with the burgeoning desire to tell him everything and pray he'd be able to deal with it. "It means a lot to me, but I want the sheriff to handle this."

He shook his head. "I can't make any promises."

She took his hand and brought it to her lips. "Just give him a couple of days. Please."

"We'll see," he said skeptically. "In the meantime Carly's roped me into buying tickets for some fund-raiser for children who've lost a parent. Dinner and dancing in two weeks. Are you game?"

"For dinner, yes." Erin grimaced. "Dancing, absolutely not."

"Why? I thought I cured your fear of dancing last week."

Erin smiled at the memory, wishing the teasing glow in his blue eyes would never fade. It made her feel weightless and wanted and everything good. "That was behind closed doors. I'd have a tough time explaining your version of 'bear dancing' to the Ladies' Auxiliary."

"Don't want to be seen with the Pendleton Devil, huh?"

She rolled her eyes, then caught herself when she

saw a flash of uncertainty come and go in his gaze. "That's not it at all," she said forcefully. "The idea of dancing in public gives me the shakes."

"If you say so."

Incredulous, Erin stared at him. "Garth." Her voice was full of reproof. "What do I have to say to convince you?"

He shrugged and looked away. "It's no big deal. I didn't want to go anyway."

She clutched his sleeve, hating that he obviously felt he still needed to hide behind a shield of nonchalance. "I'd like to go." His muscles were taut with tension beneath her hand. "Can't we eat dinner there, then come home?" She squeezed his arm. "Maybe do the dancing here?"

She felt a subtle easing take place within him. It was there in the way his muscles relaxed and he exhaled his breath. "Okay." His gaze finally met hers, dark and turbulent. "We can do the dancing here."

Sometimes she had a difficult time reading him. He was so complex. Every time one layer of his personality was uncovered, another appeared. She didn't know half of what was going on inside him. What she did know, though, was that she wanted him very sure of her feelings for him. No matter how things turned out in the end, she could give him that much.

"I don't think you understand how important you are to me." She smiled. "You don't even have a clue what you mean to me, do you?"

Garth lifted his hand to stroke her hair. "It's early days yet, babe," he said, and watched frustration cross her face.

It wasn't what she wanted him to say, he could tell. But he was thinking about this morning when he'd let the cat out of the bag and said he wanted to marry her. Her only response had been a soft, silky gasp, and she hadn't mentioned it since. He wondered if her reluctance stemmed from fear that he'd spoken out of passion or from her own fear of commitment to him.

"I love you," she said softly.

Stunned speechless, Garth stared at her.

"I really do." She lifted her chin. "If you're uncomfortable with it, I'm sorry. But it's true, and I want you to know it. I—"

"Ms. Lindsey, we finished the window."

The workman's voice filtered through Garth's consciousness. He couldn't have torn his eyes from Erin if he'd had to.

Twin flags of color bloomed on her cheeks. The emotions in her eyes shifted like the wind. "My timing's horrible."

Garth shook his head. Her timing was great. Anytime she wanted to say *I love you* was fine with him. He opened his mouth to reassure her.

She held up a hand. "No. Just think about what I've said. We'll talk about it later." She hesitated, looking uncertain and self-conscious as hell. "If you want to." She waved her hands nervously. "I've got to sign the order and—" She glanced at the clock and cursed softly under her breath. "It's time to pick up Luke." She gave him a weak smile and practically ran from the kitchen.

Garth was left standing there trying to absorb it. If half his mind had been more than mush, he would have reached for her and refused to let her go until she repeated her words about a hundred times. But he was too busy trying to deal with the giddy, higher-than-a-kite feeling fuzzing his brain, the punch-drunk sensation in his gut, and the insidious warmth curling around his heart.

Hell, he was too busy trying to remember to breathe. A wild euphoria, one he'd never experienced, rushed through him. *She loved him.* He crammed his fingers through his hair and laughed for the sheer joy of it. *She loved him.*

Shoving his hands in his pockets, he swaggered around the room, making plans. If she loved him, then they would get married. Soon, he thought. As soon as they could manage it. If she were amenable to the idea, then he'd go into partnership with her with the money he'd saved up and gotten from the sale of family property.

He rinsed out his coffee cup and shook his head, amazed that Erin could belong to him. It was incredible, unbelievable. A dream he'd never dared to dream, and it had come true.

He drummed his fingers on the counter and absently straightened the stack of mail. The envelope on top caught his attention.

Garth ran his finger over the return address, narrowing his eyes. A lawyer's office in Denver. Just seeing the city's name made his stomach muscles tighten. His enormous sense of well-being faded quickly.

One of the names was familiar. Garth's memory was the blessing and bane of his existence. He rarely forgot anything. That lawyer's name. He frowned. Click. Click. Click.

A scene came to him from seven years before in the bar where he'd been a bouncer. He could hear the man's voice. The man bragged a little too much, but Garth had always felt sorry for the guy. Underneath the tendency to down too many beers and wear flashy clothes, the guy was lonely, Garth knew, and he had always understood loneliness.

He remembered the man saying something about his lawyer. *Harvard graduate, Rhodes scholar. Yeah, Harrington's sharp as a tack. If you ever need a lawyer . . .*

The man's name settled like a noose around Garth's throat. Tom Calloway. Garth pulled his hand away from the envelope as if the distance could erase the name's effect on him.

He'd ended up needing a lawyer, but he hadn't gone to Harrington. He couldn't have asked the brilliant Harrington, since he'd killed Tom Calloway.

Garth closed his eyes. An all-too-familiar cold darkness settled over his soul while his mind whizzed with questions. Why was Erin getting mail from this lawyer? Had she lived in Denver? Was there any connection to—

*Stop.* He pinched the bridge of his nose hard. Erin didn't know anything about what had happened in Denver. With the exception of John Blackwell, no one in Beulah County knew for certain. Not his brothers, not his sister. And God help him, Erin would never know either.

The letter bothered him, though, reminding him of questions Erin wouldn't answer. He'd bided his time, and now the vandalism had escalated to shooting. Her safety was involved. Garth saw little choice in the matter. If Erin wouldn't give him the answers, he'd have to get them himself.

The front door whooshed open, and Luke barreled through, calling Garth's name.

Looking up, he prepared himself for a nonstop commentary on Luke's discovery of the day. Uneasiness ate at him, but he shook it off and wiped away his scowl. He knew what he had to do.

Garth stared at his phone. In one sense it would be an invasion of Erin's privacy to call Harrington. But if the lawyer could help them find the person behind the vandalism, shouldn't he take the chance?

Although he respected Erin's right to privacy, he wished she trusted him enough that she didn't feel it necessary to hide so much. His chest tightened at the thought. His Erin seemed to need to hide quite a bit from him.

The indecision ate at him. He rubbed a hand over his face. Lord, how to decide? So many factors rushed through his mind—privacy, respect, trust—but the most pressing was Erin's safety. Garth grimly shook his head. None of the other issues would be worth a flip if Erin or Luke got hurt. He just couldn't risk their safety.

He checked the clock. Denver was an hour behind Beulah County, so someone should still be in the office. After getting the lawyer's number from information, Garth punched the appropriate numbers and waited.

"Harrington, Fitzgerald, and Simmons," the receptionist's voice answered.

"I'm calling from Beulah County about Erin Lindsey. I need to speak with Mr. Harrington."

"Oh, you must be Sheriff Blackwell. Mr. Harrington left some information. Let's see."

Garth tried to break in, hearing the muffled rustling of papers. "I'm not—"

"Here it is. The man who leased the property before Ms. Lindsey took residence was Walter Terry. One sixteen-year-old son named Randall. According to this file, his wife has since died. Mr. Harrington made a note that Mr. Terry was very disappointed when his lease wasn't renewed."

Garth's mind clicked through the possibilities. "Do you have a forwarding address for them?"

The receptionist gave it, citing Danville as the town.

"That's just one county away," he muttered, more to himself than to her.

"I hope this information will help," the receptionist said. "We're sorry we don't have more. I believe Mr. Harrington already told you we haven't received any calls from Erin's father's business associates during the last two years."

Garth frowned. "I understood that her father was dead."

"Well, yes, but—" The receptionist sounded uncomfortable. "Mr. Calloway is dead, but, as you know, some of his business associates hounded Ms. Calloway, I mean Ms. Lindsey, after his death. I'm sure that was part of the reason she . . ."

Garth didn't hear any more. The woman kept talking and talking, but he couldn't distinguish the words. His hands began to shake. *Erin Calloway*.

He couldn't breathe. The familiar room took on an atmosphere of unreality. His stomach clenched in bitter nausea. Still the woman's voice kept on.

"Mr. Blackwell." The receptionist's distressed voice barely penetrated the black fog around him. "Mr. Blackwell, are you there?"

He forced himself to take a sip of air. "Thank you for the information." He gently replaced the receiver, keeping his hand on the phone.

His mind, as always, latched on to Erin. As if a knife stabbed into his flesh, through his ribs, all the way to his foolish heart, pain, physical and emotional, consumed him. He squeezed his eyes shut, emitting a low groan.

He had *never* felt such agony. Never. Why had he fallen for her? God help him. Of all people, why her?

Rage, familiar and self-destructive, rolled through him like a tidal wave. *Fool*, the devil on his shoulder cried. *Fool!*

Garth roared at the injustice of it; his wounded cry was so primal, an animal could have made it. Again and again he cursed himself. Then his fingers tightened around that damned phone, and in one swift violent movement he jerked it out of the wall and threw it across the room.

# TWELVE

She hadn't heard from him in three days.

Erin gave the swollen, cloudy sky another glance and led Rapunzel into the barn. She'd picked up the phone to call Garth last night, but reticence won over longing, and she'd hung up without dialing.

The air carried the smell of horseflesh and the metallic scent of impending rain. Rapunzel whickered at her, giving a playful toss of her chestnut head.

Erin smiled in spite of the underlying unhappiness she'd been struggling with. "Want to run, do you?" She stroked Rapunzel's velvet-soft nose. "Maybe tomorrow. Can't have all you pregnant ladies standing out in the cold rain."

Wind slapped at Erin's parka as she led the rest of the mares in from the pasture. The first fat raindrop plopped on her forehead as she made her final trip to the barn. A deluge of raindrops hit the roof, creating a minor roar. Erin was glad she'd followed her instincts. It would be a cold, drenching rain, just this side of sleet, the kind that soaked clear through to the bone and made her feel old. A shiver ran through her, and she rubbed her arms.

The barn door burst open. She jerked, thinking the wind was responsible, but a millisecond later Garth appeared in the doorway. He was dressed as usual in denims and black leather jacket, but Erin instantly sensed something different about him. It wasn't his overly alert posture. He was always alert. It wasn't his firm, unsmiling mouth. She knew he rarely smiled.

She met his gaze and her heart almost stopped. It was his eyes. There was a frightening, unholy light in them. And instead of the warmth she'd come to expect, now there was ice.

Another shiver passed through her. She swallowed over a lump of dread and searched for something, anything to say to break the intensity of his gaze. "You're drenched," she finally said inanely. "I bet you're freezing. Let me get an umbrella." She turned toward the tiny tack room. "We can go to the house, and I can make some—"

His hand fell on her shoulder, instantly silencing her.

"Blackwell's got your vandal in custody."

She whipped around. "Who?"

His gaze flicked over her. "A teenager named Randy Terry. His father leased the farm before you came. They've had some bad luck since then, and Randy needs to blame somebody, so he picked you."

Confusion and relief mingled. She never would have guessed. Erin ran her hand through her hair, absorbing the information. "I didn't know much about the tenants. The lawyer handled all that." She looked up at Garth. "What do we do now?"

"You need to decide whether or not to press charges."

"He's a teenager?" She frowned.

Garth nodded. "You don't have to decide right now."

She folded her arms over her chest. "Well, I guess that's good." He still stood there tensely. Not one bit of relief softened his face. Her wariness turned to something stronger as she watched him and waited.

"We need to talk." His voice was rusty, and the space around him seemed to snap and crackle with the emotions he was holding back.

She bit her lip, feeling a sense of dread. Time to pay the piper. Erin wondered how much he knew. "Okay," she managed to say. "Let me get the umbrella and—"

"Not here." Single-minded determination pulsed from him. "I want us to go to my cabin."

Her heart thumped harder in her chest. She shook her head. "Luke will be here soon. I-I can't."

"Carly's waiting in the house. Russ is out of town, and she said she'd stay the night."

Erin's eyes widened. "The night! I can't do that. Luke—"

"Luke knows Carly. He feels comfortable with her. You just need to call the school and tell him. Carly will keep him safe and amused. And since Randy's been caught, you don't have to worry about any more vandalism."

Erin shook her head again, feeling her choices narrow with each passing second. "Garth, I don't know." A flicker of pain passed through his eyes. It caught at her heart.

"I won't take no for an answer, Erin. We've got to talk, and it'll probably take all night."

He reminded her of a pot threatening to boil over, and though she knew he would never hurt her, it scared her. Everything he didn't know about her hung over her head like a guillotine. How much did he know? *How much?*

She didn't want to go, didn't want to face his questions or recriminations. If she'd cared less for him, she would have refused. But God help her, she loved him, and if this was what he wanted, then she'd do it. Erin rubbed her right temple. "All right," she said softly, her hopes being snuffed out like candles. "I'll go."

It took only a few minutes to call Luke and leave instructions with Carly. If Garth's sister sensed anything was amiss, and Erin was certain she did, she covered it well with cheerful chatter. Carly's only giveaway was a gentle, reassuring squeeze to Erin's shoulder right before Erin followed Garth out the door.

During the drive Garth was tight-lipped and silent, stewing, it seemed. Erin was lost in the sensation of being in the eye of a hurricane. Feeling raw and vulnerable, she battened down the hatches on her emotions in preparation for what was coming.

When Garth stopped, she immediately opened her door and got out of the car, wanting to escape the excruciating tension if only for a moment. He opened the door to the cabin. The cabin didn't seem nearly as cozy as it had during her other visits here. As she walked into the den, sensual images echoed across her brain one after the other. She remembered the way his skin had felt, the way he looked at her, and the way his voice had caressed her.

"How long have you known?" His voice was tempered steel behind her.

The warm, loving images fled. Erin closed her eyes and took a deep, fortifying breath. She understood what he was asking. No further explanation was needed. "Since that first night when the deputy sent you. It was your name. I knew when you told me your name."

He moved to stand in front of her, facing her, making her meet his gaze. "All this time."

"You want explanations?" She shook her head. "You want it to make sense? Well, it doesn't and it never has. I felt something for you from the very beginning and I fought it and fought you." She pointed her finger at him. "But you wouldn't take no for an answer. You kept coming around."

He looked at her with narrowed eyes. "Maybe I would have stopped if you'd clued me in on your real name, Ms. Calloway."

"My *real* name isn't Calloway anymore. Shall I show you my papers?"

His nostrils flared. "What I want to know is when were you going to tell me. When?"

Her defensiveness edged toward anger. While she hated how hurt Garth was, this whole situation had been impossible for her too.

"Never."

A look of outraged surprise suffused his face. "Never?"

Unable to bear the accusation pumping from him, she turned away. "I knew you'd find out sometime. And just how could I bring it up?" She waved a hand. "After we made love, I guess I could have said, 'Oh, by the way, Garth, I wish I hadn't driven my father nuts. Then maybe he wouldn't have murdered your boss or shot' "—her voice broke, but she swallowed hard and kept on—" 'you. And maybe you wouldn't have had to kill him.' "

Garth swore. "Wait a minute. We've been over

this before. You're not still blaming yourself for your father's death, are you?"

The silence was telling. Garth watched Erin, her stiff movements and trembling voice undercut his anger. Her tears were already threatening, and he could tell she was mortified by them. She swiped at her cheeks, and his heart clutched. "You're crazy."

She glared at him. "I am not crazy. You didn't see him when I told him I was pregnant. He wouldn't speak to me. Wouldn't even look at me. It was as if I had died." She drew in a shaky breath. "I think he would have been happier if I had."

A torrent of emotions, too many to name or dissect, flooded him. He ran a hand through his hair. "Hell."

"Intellectually I know it's not my fault," she said in a voice vibrating with misery. "But every time I think about it, I remember what sent him over the—"

"Stop it!" Garth covered her mouth. By the look in her wide eyes, he was scaring her, but he couldn't bear to hear it. "You had no control over your father. He was an adult who made his own choices. Nobody *made* him leave the house with a loaded gun. Nobody." He took a deep breath. "Tom Calloway set everything into motion that night, not you."

"You're right." She pressed her fingers to her forehead. "I know you're right. Some days I feel like I've almost reached a peace about it." She lifted her shoulders. "But other days my feelings don't always follow what my mind is telling me."

He slid his hands to her shoulders. "Then you've got to try a little harder. Your father was headed down. His business associates were crooks. He was drinking too much, and he'd pretty much abandoned you."

She stared into space as if remembering. "It happened after my mother died. He seemed to lose his way without her."

"I know what you're talking about," Garth said quietly. "The same kind of thing happened to my dad, remember?"

"Yes. I remember." She sighed. "I'm sorry my father shot you, Garth." Her eyes welled. "I'm so sorry."

"Erin." He pulled her to him, frustrated and confused. He hadn't planned on this. He'd counted on his anger carrying him through. And he still felt angry, still wanted answers. "Why didn't you tell me?"

She tore away from him. "I don't know. In the beginning I was trying to protect Luke. After a while I started feeling things for you. You made it easy to forget." She looked at the ceiling as if seeking something from heaven. "Lord knows, I wanted to forget. I wanted it to be in the past. And then"— she pressed her lips together, appearing to gather her resolve—"it seemed like all I wanted was you."

His heart stopped. It must have. He couldn't think,

couldn't seem to speak. She'd said what he'd always wanted to hear from her, but somehow the fact that she hadn't told him about her father robbed him of his pleasure. He felt unbearable sadness. "Why didn't you tell me this week?"

Her gaze clouded. "I guess I didn't want it to end yet. I was afraid." She looked at him and bit her lip. "I'm still afraid."

Garth felt the space between them build to something more substantial, a wall. He couldn't help her with her fear. Who knew what would happen between them? Who knew if they'd be able to get beyond this? While the prospect of losing Erin tore at him, he still couldn't reconcile her relationship to the man he'd been forced to kill.

He backed away, emotionally and physically. "We've got all night. I'll start a fire."

She dipped her head in disappointment, and Garth felt a corresponding plunge in his spirits. The battle inside him raged again. He didn't want to lose her, but how could he keep her?

He took his time building the fire while Erin fixed sandwiches and coffee. He toyed with the idea of taking her home. What did he really hope to accomplish?

She carried a tray through the door, tentatively gazing at him, and he immediately dismissed the idea. "Hope this is okay," she said, setting the tray down on an end table.

"It's fine." Garth remained seated and took a sandwich from the pile despite the fact that he wasn't hungry. "Thanks."

Erin didn't bother to pretend that she could down even a bite. She wandered around the room. "Why did my father buy a horse farm so close to yours?"

Garth swallowed a sip of hot coffee, feeling the burn all the way down. "We were shooting the breeze one day and he said he'd like to buy some property. I told him about Silver Creek. He never said anything to me. And since I don't make a practice of reading the real-estate-title information in the newspaper, I never realized he'd bought it."

Erin nodded. "It makes sense."

Garth gave up on the sandwich and tossed it on the plate. "You got any more questions?"

Staring into the fire, she knitted her fingers together. "Did he die quickly?"

A long pause followed her question, but Erin didn't look at Garth. She couldn't.

"Instantly. He never knew what hit him."

The flame crackled and hissed. "What about you? Was your"—she grimaced—"what about your wound?"

Restless, Garth stood. "I lost some blood. Had to stay in the hospital overnight. I was never charged with anything."

She nodded, wondering what that long night had been like.

"Did you wish they'd arrested me and tried me for murder?"

Her head shot up and she finally met his gaze. "No. I was too dazed." She shook her head. "Too guilty. And there was no one to help with the funeral arrangements except the lawyer. Then I had to make a decision about the baby."

A shadow crossed his face. He struggled to contain his emotions, she could tell.

"Did you consider getting an abortion?"

"For about ten seconds, but I couldn't." She shrugged, remembering how confused she'd been. "I thought about adoption. Once I felt him move, there was no choice in the matter. It was this little flutter." She smiled briefly at the sweet memory. There'd been so few happy moments. "I wasn't even showing yet, but I think I must have kept my hand on my abdomen for an hour waiting for it to happen again.

"What I really needed was a place to stay. I was still under eighteen, so I ended up living in a supervised home for unwed mothers until he was born. Money wasn't the problem. I just didn't have anybody—no relatives, no friends." She sighed. "Nobody. And that's the way it's been." Plucking up her courage, Erin looked him straight in the eye and laid her heart on a platter. "Till you."

Garth looked away.

Erin closed her eyes for a moment, fighting tears. They'd come so far and now they talked as if they were strangers. "You can hardly bear to look at me," she whispered.

His gaze snapped back to her. Anger and wanting fought for dominion in him. She saw flashes of his emotions come and go, felt the tearing indecision inside him, and thought about begging.

Heedless of his don't-touch-me air, she moved closer until she stood directly in front of him. "What do you think when you look at me, Garth? Tell me." When he didn't reply, desperation and recklessness swelled inside her. What did she have to lose? "Do you remember the other time I was here? When you look at me, do you remember how we made love? Do you remember how much I wanted you? Do you think about how much I love you?"

When he still didn't respond, she began to shake. Her voice broke. "I can't make you want me if you're thinking about who my fa—"

"Damn you Erin!" At that moment Garth wished with every fiber of his being that Erin were someone else. It mattered that she was Tom Calloway's daughter. He hated it, but it *did* matter. Once the thrill and excitement faded between him and Erin, he feared that she would look at him with revulsion.

His instinct was to turn away, but his feelings for her were too strong. Something in him snapped. He moved lightning-fast, taking her in his arms, bringing her so close, his breath was warm against her face. "It isn't a matter of wanting you. It's never been a matter of wanting you, because I always have."

Erin endured the heat and hostility in his gaze. Anything was better than that vast distance separating them. Moving her hands to his shoulders, she shook her head. "I don't know if we're going to be able to settle all of this tonight. I don't know what you want from me. I just wish—" She broke off and looked down, feeling foolish.

"What?" He lifted her chin with his thumb.

"I just wish," she said, staring at him and feeling lost, "I could be what you need tonight." Her innermost desire poured from her despite her uncertainty. She touched his cheek. "I wish I could take your anger and soothe it. I wish I could turn your disappointment into hope. I wish I could take your hurt and heal it."

Garth closed his eyes. Her words struck at the heart of him. He rubbed his cheek against her hand. She seemed to know what he was feeling without him saying a word. She made him ache and want. He opened his eyes to look at her, feeling his chest tighten at the way her eyes reflected pure love. "I don't know what'll happen tomorrow," he said roughly. "But I need whatever you can give me tonight."

She blinked at his blunt admission. Slowly she rose on her tiptoes and kissed the edge of his clenched jaw. His heart hammered against his rib cage.

"You need whatever I can give?" Her voice was

a smoky whisper. "Then I'll give you everything I've got." And Erin's sweet mouth took his.

She kissed him until they were both breathless. Her hands eased his shirt from his shoulders, and he felt himself slip under the spell of her ministrations. She was moist, parted lips and sweet whispers, a balm to his pain. For once he felt no responsibility to seduce her and make her ready. She let him know by every move she made that he seduced her just by being there.

She led him to his bed and undressed him with great care, kissing every part of him she unveiled, heating him until he wasn't sure if she was a teasing vixen or an angel of pleasure. A fine sheen of sweat beaded his skin as he endured the sensuous torment of her lips on his chest and belly, then lower.

"Erin," he heard himself plead hoarsely.

Her mouth was relentless, though, and she pushed him higher and further. He gasped for air, inhaling her scent. He couldn't take any more. "Erin," he choked out. "For God's sake—"

Her mouth smothered the rest of his words in a searing kiss as she held his pulsing erection between her legs and with excruciating slowness eased him inside her hot, tight channel. He felt just a hint of her inner ripple, and it was all over for him, a mighty rush that took his breath and stopped his heart.

When he calmed, she kissed him tenderly, the way a mother kisses a child, and brushed the damp hair from his temples. All his macho bravado faded beneath her touch. His heart was stripped, bare for her. She was reaching the innermost part of him tonight, where he'd bottled up all his disappointments, hurts, and pain, and her tenderness was so sweet, he ached for it.

He should have been sated, but oddly enough her compassion only made him more hungry for her. Feeling his loins swell, he reached for her, tucking her beneath him. "Again," he muttered.

She arched beneath him, taking him in with a sigh. "Again."

For Erin the night became a series of giving and taking, of seduction and surrender. She used all her resources to try to be what Garth needed, to try to tear down the walls and give him a healing that would last beyond the night. At some moments she felt so protective of him that her actions were almost maternal. Other times it was pure passion, her female to his male.

After one union she kissed his eyelids and felt him shake. He squeezed her closely to him and began to weep. The enormity of his pain wrenched at her. She sipped at the salty tracks of his tears until her own tears fell heedlessly down her own cheeks.

They collapsed together and fell asleep. At dawn he took her one more time.

"Garth." She stared into his lost eyes, willing him to see how much she cared for him. "Love." Her voice was barely a gasp.

He grimaced as if in pain. "Say it again, Erin."

The pleading note in his voice undid her, and she chanted the word again and again until she was hoarse and flying to the stars.

The night hadn't passed without a heavy cost to both of them, Erin realized when she took her turn in the shower. Her knees were weak, her body was dotted with burns from his beard, and more importantly she hadn't given a second thought to contraception. Not real bright, she thought, for someone who'd experienced the unwed-mother routine firsthand.

She could only hope someone up there would give her a break this time. Although the idea of carrying Garth's baby appealed to her, she harbored no false illusions about the difficulty of single motherhood.

What frightened her most was the fragility she felt. She hadn't comprehended what she was giving away last night. It had been far more than sex. She'd given Garth herself, and if he ended up finding her wanting, she'd be left in a vacuum no one else could fill.

Grabbing hold of the tiny shred of composure she still had, she dressed, ignoring her physical and emotional twinges. She pushed open the bathroom door, and the smell of fresh-perked coffee wafted through the air.

She made her way to the kitchen and poured herself a cup with cream and a heaping spoonful of sug-ar.

"I'll take you home after you finish that," Garth said from behind her.

Erin stiffened. "Is this it, then?"

A long silence followed, too long for her rocky emotional state. She turned around. "Answer me. Did last night mean nothing to you? Is it over between us now?"

Garth looked as raw as she felt. In fact she'd have to say he looked worse. His eyes were bloodshot, his mouth was set in an unhappy line, and for once he didn't seem to know what to do with his hands. He rested them on his hips, moved to hook his thumbs through his belt loops, then, seeming to give up, he shoved them in his pockets.

"It's too soon, Erin. I wanted things to be differ-ent with you. I wanted you to be separate from the ugliness of my past." He shook his head. "I guess I wanted too much."

"And what if I need you no matter what has hap-pened in our pasts? What if I love you so much there aren't enough words for it?"

He rubbed his hand over his face. "I don't know."

A knot formed in her throat, and her eyes started to burn. "Is it me? Is it because I'm Tom Calloway's daughter?" She swallowed hard. "Is it because every time you look at me, you think of him?"

His gaze veered away, and Erin's heart sank. It

was obvious that her worst fears were realized. Garth couldn't look at her without feeling all the emotional uproar connected with her father.

Looking up, he moved closer to her and started to take her shoulders in his hands, but seemed to think better of it.

Erin bit her lip.

He closed his eyes for a moment. "What you gave me last night. Nobody"—he lifted a hand and met her gaze—"nobody's ever done that for me. I don't know what to say."

"How about 'I love you'?" she whispered.

"I do." He was deadly serious. "I love you."

"Then we can—"

He shook his head, and Erin's spirits took another plunge. The seesaw effect left her confidence in tatters.

"I can't—" He ran an unsteady hand through his hair. "I can't live with seeing you and knowing there's nothing I can do to change what happened. I'd spend every minute wondering when you're going to wake up to the truth and look at me with hate instead of love."

As if he read her protest before she voiced it, he finally touched her, covering her mouth.

Erin felt a heavy sensation that seemed to crush the breath from her lungs. She knew what he was going to say. She also knew she wouldn't be able to change his mind.

She wanted to cover her ears so she wouldn't hear it and close her eyes so she wouldn't see it written on his face. She wanted to scream, but the hopeless expression in his eyes made her suffer in silence. His gaze locked with hers, and Erin sensed the torment this was causing him.

"I'm sorry, Erin. I just can't be with you anymore."

The wrenching pain nearly made her double over. A broken sob escaped her tight throat.

"Erin, don't—"

Stumbling backward, she shook her head, her eyes swimming with tears. "Don't you dare tell me not to cry." She hiccupped over another sob. "Don't you dare. If you're uncomfortable with it, that's just too bad. *I hurt*." She turned and ran out the door.

# THIRTEEN

He didn't want to be here.

In his current mood Garth belonged anywhere except in a crowd of people filled with the joy of Thanksgiving. If he couldn't be with Erin, he belonged at home tending his wounds with a fifth of Jack Daniel's as medicine.

Ten days had passed since that awesome night and painful morning, and Garth was calling himself ten kinds of a fool for turning Erin away. He should have taken what she'd offered, put a ring on her finger before she blinked, and gotten her pregnant so that she'd be stuck with him.

At the time, though, he'd felt as if someone had put his heart and soul through a meat grinder, and his dependence on Erin had terrified him. The mere thought of being with her and waiting for her to come to her senses only to dump him had been too much for him to bear.

The passing of a few days gave him an entirely different perspective. Maybe she'd really meant it when she'd said "I love you." A few more days and he was wondering what kind of arrogant SOB he was for telling her he couldn't be with her, for hurting her that way.

Now, on the tenth day, he craved the sight of her smile so much that he would have traded his soul for a glimpse of her.

That tore it, he thought. This couldn't continue. He would go home tonight and try to come up with a way to tell Erin how he felt . . . or die trying. Tomorrow he'd call a florist and find out if he could get some lilies. She loved lilies, she'd said when explaining why she'd made an exception in letting Luke give the mares names of fairy-tale characters. Tomorrow he'd go to her. Tomorrow and not one day later.

His sister, Carly, had dragged him out tonight, hoping to distract him, he knew. So far all he'd done was glare at every blond woman because she wasn't Erin.

Russ Bradford interrupted his thoughts. "The chicken's not bad."

Garth glanced at his plate, then at his brother-in-law, Russ. "Guess I'm not hungry."

"Hmmm." Russ tugged at the knot of his tie.

They were seated at a round banquet table with

Carly, Daniel, Troy, Jarod, Augusta Winfree, and Sara Kingston. The room was filled with people who'd purchased tickets to the Thanksgiving dinner and dance to benefit the children-who'd-lost-a-parent charity. In the background the band was warming up.

Garth spied the women making their way back from a trip to the powder room. He noticed that Sara Kingston seemed to be dawdling more than the others. He flicked a glance over to Daniel and saw that his brother had reached the same conclusion.

"When do you think Daniel's gonna quit straddling the fence and make his move?" Russ murmured.

"He's biding his time the way you did." Garth remembered the merry chase Carly had led Russ.

Russ nearly choked on his wine. "Lord help him if he's planning on waiting two years."

One thing Garth appreciated about Russ was his unique ability to make him crack a smile during some of the grim moments of his miserable life. Despite his bone-deep misery, Garth felt the faintest twitch at the corner of his mouth. "Oh, I don't know. Judging by that red mark your collar isn't hiding, you're not in too much pain now."

Russ gave a mock glower. "Your sister," he said sternly, "will be the death of me." His lips stretched into a slow, satisfied grin. "But what a way to go!"

Garth felt a pinch of envy at the obvious love that flowed between Carly and Russ.

"I thought Carly said you'd be bringing Erin Lindsey tonight."

Garth felt his muscles tighten. "Didn't work out."

Russ shook his head in sympathy. "Better see what you can do to make it work out. You might as well give in and go easy on yourself. If you don't, you could end up having to get your butt tattooed, and let me tell you—" Russ broke off mid-stream, looking across the room. "You said Erin's not coming tonight?"

Garth nodded grimly.

"Then why did she just walk through the door?"

Garth jerked his head toward the front door and felt his heart stop. He blinked twice to make certain he wasn't wishing her into his sights. Sure enough, there she was, wearing the same dress she'd worn on his birthday. The filmy material floated down to her calves, bringing to mind all sorts of sensual memories that did wild and wonderful things to his body.

Erin was listening to Carly, whose conversation appeared to be moving at top speed, and trying to see into the darkened room.

"Too dark," he murmured, remembering her night-vision problems. He impatiently watched her make her way to the table. Too slow. He stood, tossing back his glass of wine.

Troy put a staying hand on his arm. "Hey, why don't you wait and—"

"I've already waited too long. Wish me luck, little brother."

Then he strode across the dance floor toward Erin. In the background he heard Troy grumbling. "Looks like Carly won the bet this time. We'll never hear the end of it."

Garth dismissed his brothers and the rest of the world. His mind was focused with singular intensity on the one woman who meant everything to him. In the two minutes it took him to cross the room, he thought of a thousand things to say to her. *I love you. You're the best thing that ever happened to me. Marry me.* But when he finally stood in front of her, his mind went blank. She was the sweetheart of his dreams, and he felt helpless as a newborn colt.

Meeting his gaze, she pressed her lips together in a tight little smile. He'd noticed she frequently wore that expression when she was nervous.

"I had to see you," she said in a soft voice.

Desperate for privacy, he took her hand and pulled her toward the door and out into the brisk November night. The muted sounds of music and conversation were in the background now, and an air of expectation, so heavy it was almost tangible, hung between them.

Erin rubbed her arms against the cold.

Garth immediately shrugged out of his suit coat and placed it around her shoulders.

"Thanks." She hugged his jacket to her. "I-uh left my coat inside." She took a deep breath and looked away.

Garth damned his silence. He felt all tied up. Determined not to let it go on any longer, he took the plunge. "God, I've missed you."

"Really?" Her heart was in her eyes.

"Really. Cross my heart. Since you left, I haven't been worth—" She sailed into his arms, knocking the breath from his lungs. He squeezed her tight, loving the press of her body against his. "There's so much I want to tell you, but I don't know where to start."

"I was afraid you wouldn't want me. Especially after you said—"

He covered her lips. They were soft and cool against his hand. "Hush. Please. I was a fool. I didn't know what I was saying. Everything took me by surprise. I was still reeling from finding out who your father was. I just couldn't believe you wouldn't wake up one day and hate my guts."

Erin shuddered. "Garth."

"It didn't take me long to realize I'd made the worst mistake of my life." He lifted her chin to look into her eyes. "But I didn't know how to go back to you. What if you'd changed your mind?"

Erin shook her head in frustration. "For the last ten days I've tried to change my mind about you. I was angry that you could push me aside so easily when I was willing to do anything for you." Feeling the hurt afresh, she took a step back. "Then I was angry with myself for caring too much." She pushed her hair behind her ear. "I decided I must be crazy to love someone who didn't want me."

"There's where you're right," Garth muttered, pulling her back into his arms. "And wrong."

Erin looked up at him in confusion.

"You *are* crazy to love me. I don't understand it and I probably never will. But you're wrong about me not wanting you. I've always wanted you."

Erin closed her eyes, feeling tears threaten. "Carly talked me into coming tonight. She said you were down." Feeling another lick of temper, she swatted his chest. "I hope you were miserable! Do you know how much you hurt me?"

"I'm sorry, Erin." He sucked in a deep breath. "God, I'm sorry. If it helps any, I felt like I'd been gutted. What made it worse was that I knew I'd done it to myself . . . to you."

Erin slid her hands up his arms, needing to touch him to make up for the days without him. "I almost didn't come," she whispered.

His grip tightened as if he'd never let her go again. "I'm glad you did." His voice was husky with relief. "So glad."

His tone took the edge off her anger. Erin was pretty sure temper was what had held her together during the last week. Other emotions surged through— vulnerability and wonder at the way he looked at her. "You know, you say that almost as if your life depended on it."

"It does," he said with heart-stopping conviction. "I never thought I'd feel this way about a woman, Erin, and I'm still not easy about it."

She searched his face in the darkness. "It may never be easy between us. Are you going to be able to live with that?"

"I spent a lot of time thinking this week." His gaze swept possessively over her face. "About you and me. About my past and yours." He took a deep breath. "Talking with you about how you felt guilty helped me with my own guilt. I'd always wondered if I could have done something different," he confessed. "God, I must have worked through every conceivable scenario a thousand times. Some days, though, and more of them lately, I know I did the best I could during that one split second. And I'm damn glad to be alive, Erin, and that's because of you."

Erin's heart thumped against her rib cage. Her eyes burned from the suffering she heard in his voice. She waited, sensing that he needed to say more, but he was struggling to find the words.

His brow furrowed. "I realized that I can't change what happened. I can't change what I've done. I can't change who you are. And I don't want to change you, because"—his voice deepened—"you, Erin Calloway, Erin Lindsey, and, I hope someday, Erin Pendleton, are the woman who makes my life worth living."

"Are you—are you saying you still want—"

"Marry me!"

His face was hard, implacable, and his gaze was stormy with the force of a hundred emotions she sensed swelling within him.

"Yes," she said, a flood of joy bursting through her. She lifted her hand to his cheek. "Oh, Garth, yes."

Turning his face into her palm, he closed his eyes briefly. "Be sure."

"I'm sure. And I'll be with you every day for you to see just how sure I am."

"Every day."

"Yes." The music inside swelled in volume, reminding her of one little thing she hadn't resolved. "But—"

Jaw clenched, he covered her hand with his. "But what?" His voice was hoarse.

She gave a tremulous smile. "I still can't dance. I'll try to learn," she promised earnestly.

He closed his eyes and exhaled in relief, his breath a steam of vapor in the air. Pressing his forehead to hers, he gave a rough laugh that vibrated up and down her spine. "We can work on that." He smiled, and it was like the sun coming out on a cloudy day. "I think I hear some music now."

Erin refused to think of Miss Snyder at this most beautiful moment in her life. She absolutely refused.

"Erin."

She stopped. His voice held a warning note and something else. Erin heard an unspoken "please" that dissolved her insides to melted syrup. She sighed. "It's your feet."

He hooked his hands behind her waist and put an open-mouthed kiss on her neck. Erin nearly turned to putty.

"Oh, lady," he murmured. "I can't believe you're here. Put your hands behind my neck and relax. We're just gonna sway. It'll be impossible for me to keep my hands off of you until we get home."

She snuggled against him with such trust that his heart contracted. "I love you, Erin."

"I love you too." Erin gave a little shudder and looked up at him. "Don't send me away again."

Cherishing the feel of her body close to his, Garth tightened his hold. "I won't."

After a few moments she lifted her head from his shoulder. "I need to ask you," she said hesitantly, her eyes a little wary, "just one more thing." She took a deep breath of resolve. "When you look at me, what do you see?"

Garth knew what she was asking and felt the door to his heart creak wide open for her, only her. Only Erin had full access to the nooks and crannies of his very soul. "I see the woman who holds my heart in her hand."

Erin closed her eyes, tears seeping past her eyelids.

Too moved by her artless response to do anything else, Garth stroked the wetness from her cheeks with a hand that was uncharacteristically shaky. He swallowed hard over the knot in his throat. "What do you see," he asked in a rough, choked-up voice, "when you look at me?"

"My life," she said simply. "My love."

He kissed her with all the sweet passion and emotion in his heart. He kissed her until he felt the wetness of his own tears on his cheeks. Then the Pendleton Devil closed his eyes and whispered a prayer of thanks.

# THE EDITOR'S CORNER

The bounty of six LOVESWEPTs coming your way next month is sure to put you in the right mood for the holiday season. Emotional and exciting, sensuous and scintillating, these tales of love and romance guarantee hours of unbeatable reading pleasure. So indulge yourself—there's no better way to start the celebration!

Leading our lineup is Charlotte Hughes with **KISSED BY A ROGUE**, LOVESWEPT #654—and a rogue is exactly what Cord Buford is. With a smile that promises wicked pleasures, he's used to getting what he wants, so when the beautiful new physician in town insists she won't go out with him, he takes it as a very personal challenge. He'll do anything to feel Billie Foster's soft hands on him, even dare her to give him a physical. Billie's struggle to resist Cord's dangerous temptations is useless, but when their investigation into a mystery at his family's textile mill erupts into steamy kisses under moonlit skies, she has to wonder if she's the one woman who can tame his wild heart. Charlotte's talent shines brightly in this delicious romance.

New author Debra Dixon makes an outstanding debut in LOVESWEPT with **TALL, DARK, AND LONESOME**, #655. Trail boss Zach Weston is definitely all of those things, as Niki Devlin soon discovers when she joins his vacation cattle drive. The columnist starts out interested only in getting a story, but from the moment Zach pulls her out of the mud and into his arms, she wants to scorch his iron control and play with the fire in his gray eyes. However, she believes the scandal that haunts her past can destroy his dreams of happily-ever-after—until Zach dares her to stop running and be lassoed by his love. Talented Debra combines emotional intensity and humor to make **TALL, DARK, AND LONESOME** a winner. You're sure to look forward to more from this New Face of 1993!

Do you remember Jenny Love-Townsend, the heroine's daughter in Peggy Webb's **TOUCHED BY ANGELS**? She returns in **A PRINCE FOR JENNY**, LOVESWEPT #656, but now she's all grown up, a fragile artist who finally meets the man of her dreams. Daniel Sullivan is everything she's ever wished for and the one thing she's sure she can't have. Daniel agrees that the spellbinding emotion between them can't last. He doesn't consider himself to be as noble, strong, and powerful as Jenny sketched him, and though he wants to taste her magic, his desire for this special woman can put her in danger. Peggy will have you crying and cheering as these two people find the courage to believe in the power of love.

What an apt title **FEVER** is for Joan J. Domning's new LOVESWEPT #657, for the temperature does nothing but rise when Alec Golightly and Bunny Fletcher meet. He's a corporate executive who wears a Hawaiian shirt and a pirate's grin—not at all what she expects when she goes to Portland to help bail out his company. Her plan is to get the job done, then quickly return to the fast track, but she suddenly finds herself wildly tempted to run into his arms and stay there. A family is one thing she's never had time for in her race to be the best, but with Alec tantalizing her with his long, slow kisses, she's ready to seize the happiness that has always eluded her. Joan delivers a sexy romance that burns white-hot with desire.

Please welcome Jackie Reeser and her very first novel, **THE LADY CASTS HER LURES**, LOVESWEPT #658. Jackie's a veteran journalist, and she has given her heroine, Pat Langston, the same occupation—and a vexing assignment: to accompany champion Brian Culler on the final round of a fishing contest. He's always found reporters annoying, but one look at Pat and he quickly welcomes the delectable distraction, baiting her with charm that could reel any woman in. The spirited single mom isn't interested in a lady's man who'd never settle down, though. But Brian knows all about being patient and pursues her with seductive humor, willing to wait for the prize of her passion. This delightful romance, told with plenty of verve and sensuality, will show you why we're so excited to be publishing Jackie in LOVESWEPT.

Diane Pershing rounds out the lineup in a very big way with **HEARTQUAKE**, LOVESWEPT #659. A golden-haired geologist, David Franklin prowls the earth in search of the secrets that make it tremble, but he's never felt a tremor as strong as the one that shakes his very soul when he meets Bella Stein. A distant relative, she's surprised by his arrival on her doorstep—and shocked by the restless longing he awakens in her. His wildfire caresses make the beautiful widow respond to him with shameless abandon. Then she discovers the pain he's hidden from everyone, and only her tenderness can heal him and show him that he's worthy of her gift of enduring love. . . . Diane's evocative writing makes this romance stand out.

Happy reading,

With warmest wishes,

*Nita Taublib*

Nita Taublib

Associate Publisher

P.S. Don't miss the spectacular women's novels Bantam has coming in December: **ADAM'S FALL** by Sandra Brown, a classic romance soon to be available in hardcover; **NOTORIOUS** by Patricia Potter, in which the rivalry and passion between two saloon owners becomes the rage of San Francisco; **PRINCESS OF THIEVES** by Katherine O'Neal, featuring a delightfully wicked con woman and a rugged, ruthless bounty hunter; and **CAPTURE THE NIGHT** by Geralyn Dawson, the latest Once Upon a Time romance with "Beauty and the Beast" at its heart. We'll be giving you a sneak peak at these terrific books in next month's LOVESWEPTs. And immediately following this page, look for a preview of the exciting women's fiction from Bantam *available now!*

# *Susan Johnson*

Nationally bestselling author of
**SINFUL** and **SILVER FLAME**

# *Outlaw*

*Susan Johnson's most passionate and richly textured
romance yet, OUTLAW is the sizzling story of a fierce
Scottish border lord who abducts his sworn enemy, a
beautiful English woman—only to find himself a captive
of her love.*

"Come sit by me then." Elizabeth gently patted
the rough bark beside her as if coaxing a small child
to an unpleasant task.

He should leave, Johnnie thought. He shouldn't
have ridden after her, he shouldn't be panting like
a dog in heat for any woman . . . particularly for
this woman, the daughter of Harold Godfrey, his
lifelong enemy.

"Are you afraid of me?" She'd stopped running
now from her desire. It was an enormous leap of
faith, a rash and venturesome sensation for a woman who'd always viewed the world with caution.

"I'm not afraid of anything," Johnnie answered,
unhesitating confidence in his deep voice.

"I didn't think so," she replied. Dressed like a reiver in leather breeches, high boots, a shirt open at the throat, his hunting plaid the muted color of autumn foliage, he looked not only unafraid but menacing. The danger and attraction of scandalous sin, she thought—all dark arrogant masculinity. "My guardsmen will wait indefinitely," she said very, very quietly, thinking with an arrogance of her own, There. That should move him.

And when he took that first step, she smiled a tantalizing female smile, artless and instinctive.

"You please me," she said, gazing up at him as he slowly drew near.

"*You* drive me mad," Johnnie said, sitting down on the fallen tree, resting his arms on his knees and contemplating the dusty toes of his boots.

"And you don't like the feeling."

"I dislike it intensely," he retorted, chafing resentment plain in his voice.

He wouldn't look at her. "Would you rather I leave?"

His head swiveled toward her then, a cynical gleam in his blue eyes. "Of course not."

"Hmmm," Elizabeth murmured, pursing her lips, clasping her hands together and studying her yellow kidskin slippers. "This *is* awkward," she said after a moment, amusement in her voice. Sitting up straighter, she half turned to gaze at him. "I've never seduced a man before." A smile of unalloyed innocence curved her mouth. "Could you help me? If you don't mind, my lord," she demurely added.

A grin slowly creased his tanned cheek. "You play the ingenue well, Lady Graham," he said, sitting upright to better meet her frankly sensual gaze. His pale blue eyes had warmed, restoring a goodly measure of his charm. "I'd be a damned fool to mind," he said, his grin in sharp contrast to the curious affection in his eyes.

Exhaling theatrically, Elizabeth said, "Thank you, my lord," in a blatant parody of gratitude. "Without your assistance I despaired of properly arousing you."

He laughed, a warm-hearted sound of natural pleasure. "On that count you needn't have worried. I've been in rut since I left Edinburgh to see you."

"Could I be of some help?" she murmured, her voice husky, enticing.

He found himself attentively searching the ground for a suitable place to lie with her. "I warn you," he said very low, his mouth in a lazy grin, "I'm days past the need for seduction. All I can offer you is this country setting. Do you mind?"

She smiled up at him as she put her hand in his. "As long as you hold me, my lord, and as long as the grass stains don't show."

He paused for a moment with her small hand light on his palm. "You're very remarkable," he softly said.

"Too candid for you, my lord?" she playfully inquired.

His long fingers closed around her hand in an act of possession, pure and simple, as if he would keep this spirited, plain-speaking woman who startled him. "Your candor excites me," he said. "Be warned," he murmured, drawing her to her feet. "I've been wanting you for three days' past; I won't guarantee finesse." Releasing her hand, he held his up so she could see them tremble. "Look."

"I'm shaking *inside* so violently I may savage you first, my lord," Elizabeth softly breathed, swaying toward him, her fragrance sweet in his nostrils, her face lifted for a kiss. "I've been waiting four months since I left Goldiehouse."

A spiking surge of lust ripped through his senses, gut-deep, searing, her celibacy a singular, flamboyant ornament offered to him as if it were his duty, his obligation to bring her pleasure. In a flashing moment his hands closed on her shoulders. Pulling her sharply close, his palms slid down her back—then lower, swiftly cupping her bottom. His mouth dipped to hers and he forced her mouth open, plunging his tongue deep inside.

Like a woman too long denied, Elizabeth welcomed him, pulling his head down so she could reach his mouth more easily, straining upward on tiptoes so she could feel him hard against her, tearing at the buttons on his shirt so the heat of his skin touched hers.

"Hurry, Johnnie, please . . ." she whispered.

# *Moonlight, Madness, & Magic*

by

# Suzanne Foster, Charlotte Hughes, and Olivia Rupprecht

"A beguiling mix of passion and the occult. . . . an engaging read."
—*Publishers Weekly*
"Incredibly ingenious." —*Romantic Times*

*This strikingly original anthology by three of Loveswept's bestselling authors is one of the most talked about books of the year! With more than 2.5 million copies of their titles in print, these beloved authors bring their talents to a boldly imaginative collection of romantic novellas that weaves a tale of witchcraft, passion, and unconditional love set in 1785, 1872, and 1992.*

*Here's a look at the heart-stopping prologue . . . .*

OXFORD VILLAGE, MASSACHUSETTS — 1690 Rachael Deliverance Dobbs had been beautiful once. The flaming red hair that often strayed from her morning cap and curled in wispy tendrils about her face had turned more than one shopkeeper's head. Today, however, that red hair was tangled and filthy and fell against her back and shoulders like a tattered woolen shawl.

Prison had not served her well.

"The woman hath *witchcraft* in her," an onlooker spat out as Rachael was led to the front of the meeting house, where a constable, the governor's magistrate, and several of the town selectmen waited to decide her fate. Her ankles were shackled in irons, making her progress slow and painful.

Rachael staggered, struggling to catch her balance as the magistrate peered over his spectacles at her. Clearing his throat, the magistrate began to speak, giving each word a deep and thunderous import. "Rachael Deliverance Dobbs, thou hast been accused by this court of not fearing the Almighty God as do thy good and prudent neighbors, of preternatural acts against the citizenry of Oxford, and of the heinous crime of witchcraft, for which, by the law of the colony of Massachusetts, thou deservest to die. Has thou anything to say in thy defense?"

Rachael Dobbs could barely summon the strength to deny the charges. Her accusers had kept her jailed for months, often depriving her of sleep, food, and clean water to drink. In order to secure a confession, they'd whipped her with rawhide and tortured her with hideous instruments. Though she'd been grievously injured and several of her ribs broken, she'd given them nothing.

"Nay," she said faintly, "I know not of which ye speak, m'lord. For as God is my witness, I have been wrongly accused."

A rage quickened the air, and several of the spectators rose from their seats. "Blasphemy!" someone cried. "The witch would use *His* name in vain?"

"Order!" The magistrate brought his gavel down. "Let the accused answer the charges. Goody Dobbs, it is said thou makest the devil's brew of strange plants that grow in the forest."

"I know not this devil's brew you speak of," Rachael protested. "I use the herbs for healing, just as my mother before me."

"And thou extracts a fungus from rye grass to stop birthing pains?" he queried.

"I do not believe a woman should suffer so, m'lord."

"Even though the Good Book commands it?"

"The Good Book also commands us to use the sense God gave us," she reminded him tremulously.

"I'll not tolerate this sacrilege!" The village preacher slammed his fist down on the table, inciting the onlookers into a frenzy of shouting and name-calling.

As the magistrate called for order, Rachael turned to the crowd, searching for the darkly handsome face of her betrothed, Jonathan Nightingale. She'd not been allowed visitors in jail, but surely Jonathan would be here today to speak on her behalf. With his wealth and good name, he would quickly put an end to this hysteria. That hope had kept her alive, bringing her comfort even when she'd learned her children had been placed in the care of Jonathan's housekeeper, a young woman Rachael distrusted for her deceptive ways. But that mattered little now. When Jonathaan cleared her name of these crimes, she would be united with her babes once again. How she longed to see them!

"Speak thou for me, Jonathan Nightingale?" she cried, forgetting everything but her joy at seeing him. "Thou knowest me better than anyone. Thou knowest the secrets of my heart. Tell these people I am not what they accuse me. Tell them, so that my children may be returned to me." Her voice trembled with emotion, but as Jonathan glanced up and met her eyes, she knew a moment of doubt. She didn't see the welcoming warmth she expected. Was something amiss?

At the magistrate's instruction, the bailiff called Jonathan to come forward. "State thy name for the court," the bailiff said, once he'd been sworn in.

"Jonathan Peyton Nightingale."

"Thou knowest the accused, Goody Dobbs?" the magistrate asked.

Jonathan acknowledged Rachael with a slow nod of his head. "Mistress Dobbs and I were engaged to be married before she was incarcerated," Jonathan told the magistrate. "I've assumed the care of her children these last few months. She has no family of her own."

"Hast thou anything to say in her defense?"

"She was a decent mother, to be sure. Her children be well mannered."

"And have ye reason to believe the charges against her?"

When Jonathan hesitated, the magistrate pressed him. "Prithee, do not withhold information from the court, Mr. Nightingale," he cautioned, "lest thee find thyself in the same dire predicament as the accused. Conspiring to protect a witch is a lawful test of guilt."

Startled, Jonathan could only stare at the stern-faced tribunal before him. It had never occured to him that his association with Rachael could put him in a hangman's noose as well. He had been searching his soul since she'd been jailed, wondering how much he was morally bound to reveal at this trial. Now he saw little choice but to unburden himself.

"After she was taken, I found this among her things," he said, pulling an object from his coat pocket and unwrapping it. He avoided looking at Rachael, anticipating the stricken expression he would surely see in her eyes. "It's an image made of horsehair. A woman's image. There be a pin stuck through it."

The crowd gasped as Jonathan held up the effigy. A woman screamed, and even the magistrate drew back in horror.

Rachael sat in stunned disbelief. An icy fist closed around her heart. How could Jonathan have done such a thing? Did he not realize he'd signed her death warrant? Dear merciful God, if they found her guilty, she would never see her children again!

" 'Twas mere folly that I fashioned the image, m'lord," she told the magistrate. "I suspected my betrothed of dallying with his housekeeper. I fear my temper bested me."

"And was it folly when thou gavest Goodwife Brown's child the evil eye and caused her to languish with the fever?" the magistrate probed.

" 'Twas coincidence, m'lord," she said, imploring him to believe her. "The child was ill when I arrived at Goody Brown's house. I merely tried to help her." Rachael could see the magistrate's skepticism, and she whirled to Jonathan in desperation. "How canst thou doubt me, Jonathan?" she asked.

He hung his head. He was torn with regret, even shame. He loved Rachael, but God help him, he had no wish to die beside her. One had only to utter the word *witch* these days to end up on the gallows. Not that Rachael hadn't given all of them cause to suspect her. When he'd found the effigy, he'd told himself she must have been maddened by jealousy. But truly he didn't understand her anymore. She'd stopped going to Sunday services and more than once had induced him to lie abed with her on a Sabbath morn. "Methinks thou hast bewitched me as well, Rachael," he replied.

Another gasp from the crowd.

"Hanging is too good for her!" a woman shouted.

"Burn her!" another cried from the front row. "Before she bewitches us all."

Rachael bent her head in despair, all hope draining from her. Her own betrothed had forsaken her, and his condemnation meant certain death. There was no one who could save her now. And yet, in the depths of her desolation, a spark of rage kindled.

"So be it," she said, seized by a black hysteria. She was beyond caring now, beyond the crowd's censure or their grace. No one could take anything more from her than had already been taken. Jonathan's engagement gift to her, a golden locket, hung at her neck. She ripped it free and flung it at him.

"Thou shall have thy desire, Jonathan Nightingale," she cried. "And pay for it dearly. Since thou hast consigned me to the gallows and stolen my children from me, I shall put a blood curse on thee and thine."

The magistrate pounded his gavel against the table, ordering the spectators to silence. "Mistress Dobbs!" he warned, his voice harsh, "I fear thou hast just sealed thy fate."

But Rachael would not be deterred. Her heart was aflame with the fury of a woman betrayed. "Hear me good, Jonathan," she said, oblivious of the magistrate, of everyone but the man she'd once loved with all her being. "Thou hast damned my soul to hell, but I'll not burn there alone. I curse the Nightingale seed to a fate worse than the flames of Hades. Your progeny shall be as the living dead, denied the rest of the grave."

Her voice dropped to a terrifying hush as she began to intone the curse. "The third son of every third son shall walk the earth as a creature of the night, trapped in shadows, no two creatures alike. Stripped of humanity, he will howl in concert with demons, never to die, always to wander in agony, until a woman entraps his heart and soul as thee did mine—"

"My God, she is truly the devil's mistress!" the preacher gasped. A cry rose from the crowd, and several of them surged forward, trying to stop her. Guards rushed to block them.

"Listen to me, Jonathan!" Rachael cried over the din. "I've not finished with thee yet. If that woman should find a way to set the creature free, it will be at great and terrible cost. A sacrifice no mortal woman would ever be willing to make—"

She hesitated, her chin beginning to tremble as hot tears pooled in her eyes. Glistening, they slid down her cheeks, burning her tender flesh before they dropped to the wooden floor. But as they hit the planks, something astonishing happened. Even

Rachael in her grief was amazed. The teardrops hardened before everyone's eyes into precious gems. Flashing in the sunlight was a dazzling blue-white diamond, a blood-red ruby, and a brilliant green emerald.

The crowd was stunned to silence.

Rachael glanced up, aware of Jonathan's fear, of everyone's astonishment. Their gaping stares brought her a fleeting sense of triumph. Her curse had been heard.

"Rachael Dobbs, confess thy sins before this court and thy Creator!" the magistrate bellowed.

But it was too late for confessions. The doors to the courtroom burst open, and a pack of men streamed in with blazing pine torches. "Goody Brown's child is dead of the fits," they shouted. "The witch must burn!"

The guards couldn't hold back the vigilantes, and Rachael closed her eyes as the pack of men engulfed her. She said a silent good-bye to her children as she was gripped by bruising hands and lifted off the ground. She could feel herself being torn nearly apart as they dragged her from the meeting room, but she did not cry out. She felt no physical pain. She had just made a pact with the forces of darkness, and she could no longer feel anything except the white-hot inferno of the funeral pyre that would soon release her to her everlasting vigil.

She welcomed it, just as she welcomed the sweet justice that would one day be hers. She would not die in vain. Her curse had been heard.

"Fayrene Preston has an uncanny ability to create intense atmosphere that is truly superb."
—*Romantic Times*

# *Satin and Steele*
by
# Fayrene Preston

SATIN AND STEELE *is a classic favorite of fans of Fayrene Preston. Originally published under the pseudonym Jaelyn Conlee, this novel was the talented Ms. Preston's first ever published novel. We are thrilled to offer you the opportunity to read this long-unavailable book in its new Bantam edition.*

Skye Anderson knew the joy and wonder of love—as well as the pain of its tragic loss. She'd carved a new life for herself at Dallas' Hayes Corporation, finding security in a cocoon of hard-working days and lonely nights. Then her company is taken over by the legendary corporate raider James Steele and once again Skye must face the possibility of losing everything she cares about. When Steele enlists her aid in organizing the new company, she is determined to prove herself worthy of the challenge. But as they work together side by side, Skye can't deny that she feels more than a professional interest in her new boss—and that the feeling is mutual. Soon she would have to decide whether to let go of her desire for Steele once and for all—or risk everything for a second chance at love.

And don't miss these heart-stopping
romances from Bantam Books,
on sale in November:

## ADAM'S FALL
a new hardcover edition of the Sandra
Brown classic!

## NOTORIOUS
by Patricia Potter
The *Romantic Times* 1992
"Storyteller of the Year"

## PRINCESS OF THIEVES
by Katherine O'Neal
"A brilliant new talent bound to make her
mark on the genre." —Iris Johansen

## CAPTURE THE NIGHT
by Geralyn Dawson
"A fresh and delightful new author!
GOLD 5 stars"
—*Heartland Critiques*

and in hardcover from Doubleday

## ON WINGS OF MAGIC
a classic romance by Kay Hooper

# OFFICIAL RULES

To enter the sweepstakes below carefully follow all instructions found elsewhere in this offer.

The **Winners Classic** will award prizes with the following approximate maximum values:  1 Grand Prize: $26,500 (or $25,000 cash alternate); 1 First Prize: $3,000; 5 Second Prizes: $400 each; 35 Third Prizes: $100 each; 1,000 Fourth Prizes: $7.50 each. Total maximum retail value of Winners Classic Sweepstakes is $42,500.  Some presentations of this sweepstakes may contain individual entry numbers corresponding to one or more of the aforementioned prize levels.  To determine the Winners, individual entry numbers will first be compared with the winning numbers preselected by computer.  For winning numbers not returned, prizes will be awarded in random drawings from among all eligible entries received.  Prize choices may be offered at various levels.  If a winner chooses an automobile prize, all license and registration fees, taxes, destination charges and, other expenses not offered herein are the responsibility of the winner.  If a winner chooses a trip, travel must be complete within one year from the time the prize is awarded.  Minors must be accompanied by an adult. Travel companion(s) must also sign release of liability.  Trips are subject to space and departure availability.  Certain black-out dates may apply.

The following applies to the sweepstakes named above:

**No purchase necessary.**  You can also enter the sweepstakes by sending your name and address to:  P.O. Box 508, Gibbstown, N.J.  08027.  Mail each entry separately. Sweepstakes begins 6/1/93.  Entries must be received by 12/30/94.  Not responsible for lost, late, damaged, misdirected, illegible or postage due mail.  Mechanically reproduced entries are not eligible.  All entries become property of the sponsor and will not be returned.

**Prize Selection/Validations:**  Selection of winners will be conducted no later than 5:00 PM on January 28, 1995, by an independent judging organization whose decisions are final.  Random drawings will be held at 1211 Avenue of the Americas, New York, N.Y. 10036.  Entrants need not be present to win.  Odds of winning are determined by total number of entries received.  Circulation of this sweepstakes is estimated not to exceed 200 million.  All prizes are guaranteed to be awarded and delivered to winners.  Winners will be notified by mail and may be required to complete an affidavit of eligibility and release of liability which must be returned within 14 days of date on notification or alternate winners will be selected in a random drawing.  Any prize notification letter or any prize returned to a participating sponsor, Bantam Doubleday Dell Publishing Group, Inc., its participating divisions or subsidiaries, or the independent judging organization as undeliverable will be awarded to an alternate winner.  Prizes are not transferable.  No substitution for prizes except as offered or as may be necessary due to unavailability, in which case a prize of equal or greater value will be awarded.  Prizes will be awarded approximately 90 days after the drawing.  All taxes are the sole responsibility of the winners.  Entry constitutes permission (except where prohibited by law) to use winners' names, hometowns, and likenesses for publicity purposes without further or other compensation.  Prizes won by minors will be awarded in the name of parent or legal guardian.

**Participation:**  Sweepstakes open to residents of the United States and Canada, except for the province of Quebec.  Sweepstakes sponsored by Bantam Doubleday Dell Publishing Group, Inc., (BDD), 1540 Broadway, New York, NY 10036.  Versions of this sweepstakes with different graphics and prize choices will be offered in conjunction with various solicitations or promotions by different subsidiaries and divisions of BDD.  Where applicable, winners will have their choice of any prize offered at level won.  Employees of BDD, its divisions, subsidiaries, advertising agencies, independent judging organization, and their immediate family members are not eligible.

Canadian residents, in order to win, must first correctly answer a time limited arithmetical skill testing question.  Void in Puerto Rico, Quebec and wherever prohibited or restricted by law.  Subject to all federal, state, local and provincial laws and regulations.  For a list of major prize winners (available after 1/29/95): send a self-addressed, stamped envelope entirely separate from your entry to:  Sweepstakes Winners, P.O. Box 517, Gibbstown, NJ 08027.  Requests must be received by 12/30/94.  DO NOT SEND ANY OTHER CORRESPONDENCE TO THIS P.O. BOX.

# Don't miss these fabulous Bantam women's fiction titles

## on sale in November

## • NOTORIOUS

by Patricia Potter, author of *RENEGADE*

*Long ago, Catalina Hilliard had vowed never to give away her heart, but she hadn't counted on the spark of desire that flared between her and her business rival, Marsh Canton. Now that desire is about to spin Cat's carefully orchestrated life out of control.*

___56225-8 $5.50/6.50 in Canada

## • PRINCESS OF THIEVES

by Katherine O'Neal, author of *THE LAST HIGHWAYMAN*

*Mace Blackwood was a daring rogue—the greatest con artist in the world. Saranda Sherwin was a master thief who used her wits and wiles to make tough men weak. And when Saranda's latest charade leads to tragedy and sends her fleeing for her life, Mace is compelled to follow, no matter what the cost.*

___56066-2 $5.50/$6.50 in Canada

## • CAPTURE THE NIGHT

by Geralyn Dawson

*In this "Once Upon a Time" Romance with "Beauty and the Beast" at its heart, Geralyn Dawson weaves the love story of a runaway beauty, the Texan who rescues her, and their precious stolen "Rose."*

___56176-6 $4.99/5.99 in Canada

**Ask for these books at your local bookstore or use this page to order.**